CENTRAL OREGON WRITERS GUILD
2022 LITERARY COLLECTION

Copyright © 2022 by COWG

All rights reserved. This book or any portion thereof may not be reproduced or used in any manner whatsoever without the express written permission of the publisher except for the use of brief quotations in a book review.

Printed in the United States of America

Cover photograph by Brigitte Lewis

First Printing, 2022
ISBN 979-8-9866920-0-5
LCCN 2022915475

Central Oregon Writers Guild
www.CentralOregonWritersGuild.com

TABLE OF CONTENTS

Fiction

Query Hell	9
Smith Rock 2121	13
A Time to Die	15
Thy Daily Bread	30
Childhood Remembered	42
A Gift for Eula	52
Native-Born Immigrant	55
Hershey	62
Hope	66
It's All Relative	76
Ghosts	92
Why I Didn't Become a Cowboy	95
Diamond Sue, Oregon	109
Technical Foul	113
Harry Can't	120
Transplace	128
A Stabbing at Midnight	143
Wood Thrush	151
Seraphim	161
Learning From Birds	172
The End or the Beginning	183
The Ascent of Acer	189
The Beach	192
Your Song	202
Morney	221

Poetry

Wild Plums	12
At the Tractor Pull	27
The Parents	33
Windbreakers	40
Shallows	50
Autumn's Fleeting Love	61
Silent Echoes	75
Safe at Last	83
Ripe Berries	94
Sand Dollar Pairing	103
Friday Nights	112
Encounter	118
What's in it for the River?	126
Pandemics	140
Moonflowers	147
Peonies	150
Does the Ocean Love Me?	160
Lepus Californicus	167
Invitation	170
Happy Birthday	182
Crowning Piety	187
Unicorno	190
The Obstetrician of Iris	201
Park Bench	206
New Moon, Beloved Darkness	217
Just Enjoy	218
Bewilderment	220
Widow's Walk	227

Nonfiction

Going Home	28
Elusive Apology	34
19 Candles: Living with Fire	35
Buddha With One Ear: Becoming an Old Woman	45
Butter Tea	81
Fifteen Seconds	85
The Apothecary	97
A Date With the Hirwas	105
"A" is for Alzheimer's	116
A Solitary Tear	142
Our Roots	148
If Only	168
Canadian Lab, Eh?	208
My Uterus is in the Fridge	229

INTRODUCTION

A spirit of creativity lives in the High Desert of Central Oregon. Inspiration is everywhere, from sparkling rivers that unfurl like ribbons to sorbet sunsets over the snow-capped Cascades and obsidian evenings splattered with stars. We are lucky to be surrounded by so much beauty and a writing community who wishes to add to it with their contributions in literature. This year, thirty-seven writers share stories and poetry about the things that inspire them.

The Central Oregon Writers Guild presents our 2022 Member Anthology, filled with a diversity of voices in fiction, nonfiction, and poetry. Founded in 2002, the Guild is a nonprofit organization run entirely by volunteers. Our goal is to mutually support and advance the growth and success of our members, in all genres and skill levels, through monthly meetings, quarterly workshops, and annual events.

QUERY HELL
By Lynda Sather

Last fall, I finally finished the novel begun five years and a thousand miles ago—before my son left for college and my husband left for another woman. Writing in the solitude of my new home was a dream. Now, I'm trying to get it published. A nightmare.

I'm supposed to find a literary agent by perusing websites to find one whose field of interest matches my Great Alaska Novel. Yeah, right.

I've spent as much time on my query letter as on the entire 350-page novel. Instead of getting an agent, all I've gotten is depressed.

Every morning, I play a little game. Would I rather clean the toilet or compose a query letter? Sweep under the bed or send a query? Cull expired food from the pantry or, well, you get it.

Unfortunately, the bathroom is now spotless, the dust bunnies vanquished, and let's just say food poisoning isn't on the menu anytime soon. I am sitting at my desk *not* looking out the window wondering if the humming bird will fly by to check out the magenta bougainvillea. I am *not* thinking about what to have for dinner (stir fry with chicken) or how little is left in the checking account ($229.56).

Perusing the list of potential agents, I can tell most of them are millennials. They have to be with names like Jessica, Ashley, and Jennifer. Half the names that should have a Y at the end have double EE. Maree. Lindsee. Emilee. If the name *should* end with an E, it's been changed to a Y. Jacky. Katy. Lesley.

There's a Chloé, which rhymes with Bok Choy, which maybe I should put in my stir fry tonight. Or did I throw it out?

Cyndee with both a Y and two Es is obviously confused. I'm not querying her.

Candee with two EEs. That spurs me to investigate the freezer where a bag of M&Ms left from Halloween still lurks. With the taste of chocolate now melting in my mouth, not in my hands, I return to the desk.

Ann/Anna/Ana/Annie. Even an Annee. A-N-N-double E E. I kid you not.

And where are the male agents? Off writing wine labels, I guess. *Whimsical yet weighty with a whiff of plum underscoring an insouciant blend of herbs married to a boldly flavored, well-crafted yet lush textured cabernet.* Is it too early in the day to start drinking?

Some of the agents think they can fool me with their unisex name. Jordon. Kerry. Kelly. But I know. I've studied their photos. Very few, male or female, look over thirty. What happened to the seasoned agents who might actually connect with my story? Buried under a deluge of queries, I suspect. If these young agents would spend more time reading my submission and less time inventing silly ways to spell their name, I would probably be published by now.

But wait! Maybe I would have more luck if I changed the spelling of my name from plain old Linda with an I to Lynda with a Y. Or Lindee., with two E's. Maybe even Lyndee, LYND double EE?

I open a blank document, pour myself a glass of wine, and begin writing with renewed resolve: *Once upon a time in an urban gothic paranormal alternative universe there was a marginalized neurodivergent hopepunk transvestite vampire fleeing a drug cartel's animatronic drones while enlisting dolphins to help him/her/it search for the utopian kingdom of Atlantis rumored to be the last remaining bastion of dark chocolate in the galaxy . . .*

Hey, look. A hummingbird!

WILD PLUMS
By Ginger Dehlinger

Green dusts the scrublands
not yet the branch
when your wee white blossoms
brew olfactory bliss
more divine than sister rose.

Besotted bees
ravage your jasmine gametes,
raucous parties that spawn
blush-cheeked,
yellow-bellied orbs—
tough on the outside
succulent within.

My knife slices to the bone.
Juice from each small sacrifice
stains my fingers,
tantalizes my tongue,
fills my jars with joy.

SMITH ROCK 2121
By David Cook

I was born in the year of the great pandemic. My parents left the country with me the following year. All my life I have heard about the natural beauty of my birth homeland, but I have never seen it. My grandchildren booked me on this excursion to Central Oregon, the place of my beginning, on the occasion of my one-hundredth birthday.

The plane is in the landing phase now. I can see below me a great, straight eight-lane highway occupied with bumper-to-bumper traffic. On each side of the highway, as far as I can see, are buildings, parking lots, and houses. This must be the great metroplex of BRETT, a name the brochures describe as having been derived by combining the names of the forming towns of Bend, Redmond, Tumalo, and Terrebonne.

The airport is reported to be one of the busiest in the nation, and it takes forever to get through customs. I board my tour van, and we snake our way through the complex of airport parking lots and finally merge heading north onto the eight-lane highway I had seen earlier from the air. The driver explains that our first stop, before he drops us off at our hotels, will be the famous Smith Rock. Even though it is now dark, I see a glow on the horizon in front of us. As we get closer to the glow, I can make out what appears to be a tall, elongated cliff, the face of which is covered with pulsating-colored lights. The driver pays an entrance fee, and we park directly across from the lighted cliff face. From here I can see that the pulsating lights I could see from a distance outline the track of a roller coaster that careens and loops around the top and face of the cliff. Even over the din of the music I can hear the passengers scream as the roller coaster cars descend rapidly in a steep dive. The pulsating lights I can now tell are keeping time with rock music that's so loud I can feel it vibrating through my bones. I wonder, somewhat sarcastically, if this is why they call this place Smith Rock.

    I walk up to a railing and look down at a brightly illuminated river canyon both banks of which are covered with a slightly elevated floor. The near floor is a dance floor packed with gyrating bodies keeping time to the music. The far floor is a lounge area adorned with lighted signs featuring various craft beers. An uncovered walkway connects the two. My gaze moves to the dark ribbon between, the river itself. I stare vacantly at the scene before me. I had envisioned my homeland somewhat differently, but what should I have expected? Things do change in one hundred years.

A TIME TO DIE
A Short Story by Eric Moser

Detective Matt Malloy had run into Joseph Keep over the years in any number of joints around town. Usually the same way; Keep behind the bar answering questions, Malloy perched on a stool asking them. Asking about what transpired to leave yet another body on a beer-stained floor, in the alley behind, and in the cheap walk-up above. Malloy shook the south Florida rain from his coat and settled heavily at the bar.

"Been awhile, Detective—beer?"

"Yes, to the beer, and yes it has, happily."

"You don't like my company, Detective?" Keep slid a Bud down the bar from the cooler—his memory impeccable, or maybe for a cop it was just a safe bet.

"I don't like your answers, Keep."

"You don't have to ask."

"I like the beer."

"I'd give that to you anyway."

Malloy took a gulp of the beer, put his pad and pen on the bar top. "Shall we?"

"Fire away."

"You knew the deceased?"

"Yep."

"How long?"

"Since he arrived, November second."

Malloy raised his eyebrows and made a note in his neat block letter style. "That's pretty specific, Joe."

"It was a Monday, the first after Halloween."

"Uh-huh. How'd you know it was a Monday?"

"It was taco night. Monday's always taco night."

"Isn't that Tuesday?"

"What?"

"Taco night is Tuesday cause it's alliterative; you know, like Taco Tuesday. Has a ring."

"Allit . . . ? So, you gonna sing now?"

"What?"

"Like a jingle." Getting a blank look from Malloy he continued, "Like you was going to sing was all I meant."

Malloy took another gulp of the beer. "I don't sing, Joe. That's what you do."

Yeah, as to that, what do I ever get out of this?"

"Where's the *quo* for the *quid pro*, you're asking?"

"Sure, I guess."

"I never consider you a suspect."

"Yeah?"

"Right away that is."

"Oh? Well, to get back to the line of interrogation, here it's taco Monday and it ain't got no ring."

"It's not an interrogation, Joe, it's an inquest, and yet I still must ask, how do you know it was a Monday?"

"'Cause I asked him—Jaime—if he wanted a taco with his drink."

"Yeah?"

"He says 'No thanks,' very polite with an old chap like, 'No thanks, old chap.' Like that. Second thing he says after ordering his drink, and I won't forget that neither."

"And that was?"

"Martini, shaken and not stirred."

Malloy made a note then asked, "You act like there's something wrong with that."

"No way to make a martini if you ask me, but I think to myself *what does a limey know?*"

"Shaken?"

"Vodka."

"Anything else?"

"Yeah, vermouth and olive."

Malloy put down the pen. "I meant about the man. You say he was English?"

"He sure sounded it. Very classy. *Masterpiece Theatre* and all that. Not a day under eighty, but fit. Light on his feet for an old guy."

"Like he could handle himself?"

"I'd say especially. He was packing."

"What makes you say that?"

"I saw it once. Under his jacket—shoulder holster, small auto, thirty-two caliber I'd say, as if I knew a thing about it."

"Uh-huh. Did he carry often?"

"All the time, I think. Always wore his dinner jacket."

"Yeah?"

"Yeah, for crying out loud. White with cummerbund and black tie. But you know," Keep leaned his elbows on the bar, "it was alright somehow, the accent, the crazy outfit, his loopy drink. It was kind of cool in a way. "

"What way is that?"

"He had style. Hard to put it another way. I'll tell you what though." Keep leaned in again to quietly say, "He had a way with the ladies."

"What? You mean around here?"

Keep nodded over the detective's shoulder, to the woman approaching.

Malloy turned and watched with frank admiration Veronica Makeout—stage name, but that's the past, another story—who always walked, particularly with men watching, which was usually the case in her natural environment, as if it had nothing to do with simply getting across the room. Her evening dress—and Malloy had never seen her wear anything else, when she was wearing anything that is—reached to the floor in shimmering gold sequin that clung to her curves with a loving kindness, bigger and rounder than ever, but still in the right places.

"Detective Malloy, always a pleasure."

Malloy rose and accepted the light hug. "Under better circumstances, perhaps."

"When are they ever, Matt, when are they ever?" She sat. Keep already had a cigarette and lighter ready, "Thanks, dear."

"I'm going to have ask you a few questions, Ronnie," Malloy said gently. Her real name would go into the official file of course, but few knew it, much less used it.

Keep moved down the bar a discreet distance, found some glasses to polish.

Ronnie held up the cigarette. "You don't mind, do you, Matt?"

"It's your place."

"I hear there's a law."

"We don't enforce laws, honey, haven't in years."

"Then what's all this?"

"Appearances." He flipped to a new page in his notebook. "Shall we start?"

Ronnie waved a hand for Malloy to continue.

"How would you describe your relationship with the deceased?"

Ronnie put the cigarette down on the edge of the bar, regarding Malloy coolly. "Joe tell you that?"

"He didn't have to Ronnie."

"We were close." Her expression changed suddenly, eyes batted reflectively and Malloy suddenly realized she was about to cry. "Oh dear!" She swept the corners of her eyes and smeared the mascara some more. Malloy handed her a handkerchief. "Oh dear. I've been a mess over this." She sniffed into the hanky. "Thanks." She took a deep, shuddering breath to compose herself, picked up her cigarette and flicked off the ash. "Jaime and I," she started again and had to pause. "Ahem. . . well, we enjoyed each other's company very much. He was a gentleman."

Malloy paused with his pen, peered up at Ronnie.

"And a man," she added. She drew long on the cigarette, looking out the raindrop-teared window over the bar. "I doubt I shall ever meet the likes of him again."

Malloy gave Ronnie another moment, stared down at the blank page in his notebook.

She smiled wanly. "He paid six months in advance for a single-wide, number twelve. You could write that down."

"Uh-huh. Was he out of town much?"

"He had some business, I guess."

"Do you know what kind?"

"Matt, I don't ask the business of my renters . . . or friends. Let's see, he didn't have any unusual habits, nor kept long hours. Nothing out of the ordinary that I saw in his belongings, but you'd know that by now."

Malloy put the notebook back in his pocket. "You know it's just business."

"Sure Matt. Well, where to begin. Jaime was a man, and a good man. I don't know where he came from or what he did to wind up here at the Palmetto."

"He didn't say anything?"

"Whatever he did, he'd learned to keep it locked away, and I never asked. It's South Florida, Matt."

"Yeah, I know, Ronnie, we all have . . . something." He picked up his beer and swirled the remaining contents.

"Yeah like that. We laughed, Matt. That's what it was. He was a good dancer. He kept his liquor. He was funny." She laughed softly with a thought. "Always with the one-liners. You know, dry-like. A wit I'd say."

"Uh-huh." Malloy put down the beer. "I guess that's enough."

"Matt," Ronnie reached out, her fingertips brushing a sleeve. "Come around sometime. For old times."

Malloy stood, flipped a bill onto the counter. "For old times? Sure. Can you make sure Joe gets some of that? He complained about my generosity."

***

Back at the station Malloy had just sunk wearily behind his desk when the department lieutenant showed up at his elbow as if on cue, leaned over, hands on desk, and asked "So?"

"Not much to go on. Apparently, the gentleman was a gentleman, making the scene at the Palmetto Trailer Park and Resort."

"Huh? Not hard to do, I suppose."

"Oh, I don't know about that, lieutenant. There's still some class left here and there in the world."

"And the other perps?"

"It seems like destruction by mutual accord."

The lieutenant grinned. "God, how I love clean, effective homicides like that. No loose ends."

"Well, a motive, Lieutenant. Comes to mind, is all I'm saying."

The lieutenant stood up and gave a dismissive wave. "Say, I've got a visitor for you. A new wrinkle in the case you might say, 'cept it's all wrapped up with a bow as far as I'm concerned."

"So?"

"Been waiting in my office for you to get back."

"In your office?"

"Let's just say the interrogation room is too common for her. A bit of a lady." The lieutenant pushed the end of his nose up for emphasis. "Anyway, she's all yours." He jerked a thumb over his shoulder down the corridor to his office.

Malloy tiredly got to his feet. "You coming?"

The lieutenant was already headed in the opposite direction. "You take it Matt. I think I'd do better just to make some coffee. You'll see."

In the lieutenant's office Malloy found a trim and ancient woman, outrageously dressed for south Florida in any season in a worsted jacket and skirt. She was perched on the edge of a visitor's chair with the kind of erect carriage that can only be taught in the right schools. Standing behind her was a man, much younger but only in a relative sense. He also was remarkably dressed in a double-breasted pinstripe. He at least had a pleasant expression for the detective. The old lady gave him a hawkeyed once over.

Malloy nodded to the man and addressed the lady, "Ma'am, I'm Detective Malloy." The lady did not rise but offered her hand, palm down. Malloy felt he was expected to kiss it.

"And you are the officer in charge of the case?" She spoke in what Malloy took to be a very proper English accent.

"If we are speaking of one Jaime Vinculo, then yes."

"Charmed." She released her hand. "This," she said without bothering to turn or gesture to the younger man, "is Mister Boothroyd."

The man leaned over to offer his hand. His grip was firm, and Malloy was surprised at the rough, calloused feel. From his looks he appeared an ivy leaguer, or perhaps it was Oxford, but somehow, he got the feeling it wasn't anything so refined.

Malloy sat in the other visitor's chair and began digging out his notebook.

"That won't be necessary, Detective," the lady said.

"Hmm." He produced it anyway. "May I ask your name, ma'am."

She smiled demurely. "Julian," she held up her hand and Boothroyd produced from inside his jacket an envelope to hand to Malloy. Within was a single folded sheet with what appeared to be an official letterhead.

Startled, Malloy looked back up to the lady. "CIA, ma'am?"

"Please read it, Detective."

He did so quickly. It was a brief statement of diplomatic protocol. Slowly he replaced the letter and handed it back to Boothroyd. "This and your British accent don't prove anything."

She gave him a very slight, approving smile. "You may dial up Mister Leiter, author of the letter as you may have noted. He will verify our identity."

"He might also have come down with you, ma'am."

"It is late, and Mister Leiter has a handicap—in service to your country. I did not wish to impose so. But if it is necessary. Julian?"

Boothroyd produced two passports that Malloy took time to study. He gave them back and then asked. "May I ask the exact purpose of your trip?"

"To claim one of our own. The deceased was a foreign national and connected to Her Majesty's government."

"And my investigation?"

"Will be completed by other means."

"I see."

"Under the auspices of the FBI, you may be assured, which of course has legal purview under these circumstances."

"I suppose I am free to contact the FBI."

"Of course."

"And they will tell me that a Ms. Olivia Mansfield and a Major Q. Boothroyd are to be given every cooperation?"

"I should think they would."

"I see." Malloy put away his notebook. Settled back in his chair he regarded the old lady, who shrewdly did the same back. He began, "In the morgue are three men, victims I am suspecting of the deceased, one Senor Jaime Vinculo." Mansfield's eyes narrowed. "Each, as they appeared to be at the scene, had been armed with an automatic weapon."

"The subject however, Senor Vinculo, was discovered without a mark on him." Mansfield finished for him. "The coroner has determined death by cardiac arrest. The other three had been shot, once each. In the head."

Malloy nodded thoughtfully, "I see you have been excellently informed. Well, a man of that age," he shrugged, "the excitement."

The lady sniffed. "Exertion perhaps. I can assure you that Jaime did not die by 'excitement' or whatever you meant by that."

"Pardon me, ma'am. Now, if I may ask, since it appears that it is I who is in the dark; but each of the assailants had a mark on them that was identical . . . ?"

"You are outside the terms of the agreement, Detective."

"Am I? I am presuming of course the gentlemen in question, the apparent victims of Senor Vinculo, were not under diplomatic protection."

Mansfield sighed gently, "You refer to the tattoos on their forearms."

"Why yes, of an animal."

"Don't be coy, detective, they are of an octopus, and the significance of it I shan't be inclined to reveal."

"Each assailant," Malloy went on, the memory of the scene still sharp, "was killed by a single gunshot to the head, as you say. Between the eyes to be precise. Very precisely."

"And?"

"Most impressive for a lone, old man. At a distance, we estimated, of nearly thirty feet. Almost miraculous I'd say."

"Jaime was highly skilled."

"With the 7.65 mm Walther PPK, found in the subject's possession?"

"You find something remarkable in that?"

"I do. Very much." Glancing up he found Boothroyd giving him an approving look for the technical point, as one man to another, in the trade as it were. "West German manufacture," Malloy continued, "serial number indicates it was built in probably the year 1959."

"I shall be requiring the pistol as well, Detective. And now," she straightened further and gave an expectant look to Major Boothroyd, but it was Malloy, who rose to give her a hand up. Both the lady and chair creaked slightly. She patted his hand. "I feel, under other circumstances we might have got on, Detective Malloy, but really I have said too much already. Haven't I, Major, said too much?"

"Never mum, you are the model of discretion."

"Ha!" The Major is the model of decorum. "I am so sorry to leave it at this, Detective, but really, duty and all that."

Boothroyd already had the door open for her.

"Excuse me, ma'am," Malloy said before she was out the door. "There was another article found on the body. A personal item, it appears. And only the one, curiously."

The lady's eyes widened only slightly, but he had her interest. "Oh?"

"A cigarette lighter, rather unusual. That is, given its age."

"Perhaps not so, considering the gentleman, as you have pointed out."

"Perhaps. A Dunhill. Circa 1960s, I believe."

"I see." She gripped the doorknob and nodded to Boothroyd. "If you would, Major." Without a word he stepped out in the corridor. Mansfield closed the door and faced Malloy. "You are quite thorough, Detective. I see my initial impression is correct. You will see to it that the lighter is included in the effects."

"I will, ma'am. There is an inscription, however."

Mansfield took a deep breath. "I should hope you are not about to be impertinent, Detective."

"Never, ma'am."

"Very well. Let me spare you the suspense. The inscription reads, 'James, Always . . .'"

"Olivia." Malloy finished for her.

"Yes." Her voice had gotten rather small.

"And if my Spanish serves me Jaime may be the equivalent of the English name, James."

"Of course, it could. Quite common in both languages, I should think." She paused. "Anything else, Detective?"

"Ma'am? Not a thing. It's South Florida after all, as another grand lady has informed me this evening. I will of course check out your story."

"Of course."

"And arrange to have all effects delivered . . . ?"

"Julian will be by in the morning with details."

"Then, good evening to you, ma'am."

"Good evening, Detective." She paused. "I shall remember you, Malloy."

"I think that is meant as a good thing, Ms. Mansfield."

"It is." But she seemed to have reconsidered something, and still stood, hand on the knob.

"Ma'am?" Malloy asked.

"His name was Bond, Detective. James Bond."

And she was gone.

AT THE TRACTOR PULL
By Pam Tucker

it's boots and farm store caps
rows of vintage tractors
matched to men in overalls—

meat and potatoes men
who hitch their tractors to the sled
engage gears and begin
the crawl, some steady,
some with a bucking leap
until the growing weight
grinds like debt or drought.

By golly, all those acres
plowed, sculpting fields
that bear a season
teach a man a thing or two:
how to move ahead,
one eye turned back
to keep 'er straight,
to plug along
to pull one's load

to goose it once or twice
when the engine groans
to eke out a little more.

How to slap a hat against a leg
say *Maybe next year.*
Maybe then.

GOING HOME
By Mary Krakow

Home. The scent of oak trees tickles my nose. My friend Joanne and I spent barefoot summers picking prickly leaves from our feet. As a teen, I strolled hand-in-hand with a succession of boyfriends under oaks. I taught my young children to climb trees at my childhood home. This year, Mom moved from that house into assisted living surrounded by familiar oaks. I stay at the old house while in town visiting her.

Joanne meets me for lunch. After lunch, we visit Mom until her bridge game starts. Then we walk aimlessly as we catch up. I'm closer to Joanne than my own cousins. We're the same age, born two weeks apart. Her mother was the maid of honor at my mom's wedding. They've known each other for nearly seventy years.

A path beckons us off the residential streets and leads us under coast live oaks, over a creek, and past a school.

"What's that?" I point to a park-like setting beyond a chain wire fence.

Joanne sucks in a breath. "My word! I had no idea it was this close to your mom's."

"What?"

"Alta Mesa."

I wait for further explanation.

"Mom and Dad are buried there."

The angel statues begin to make sense. "Would you like to visit?" Her dad's recent passing was a big topic at lunch.

"You wouldn't mind?"

"Of course not." We walk with renewed purpose. I haven't seen Jo and Art in years.

They lay side by side. Simple plaques state their name, birth and death dates, service branch. Art: US Navy. Jo: US Naval Reserves.

Joanne pulls overgrown tufts of grass and talks to her parents.

I say a few words myself.

Surprisingly, our visit to Jo and Art's graves leaves us satisfied. The walk back to Mom's place is filled with lighthearted conversation, memories, and promises to stay in touch. Back at our cars we say good-bye.

Mom's bridge game won't be over for another hour. I return to my childhood home surrounded by memories. Joanne and I chasing lizards, Mom and Dad hosting Jo and Art for bridge, Jo comforting Mom at Dad's memorial service under our backyard oaks. Unlike Joanne, I can still wander around in my childhood home. One day soon, that will change, memories alone will have to sustain me. I close my eyes and inhale the distinctive scent of fallen oak leaves. The smell of home.

THY DAILY BREAD
By Gerry Pare

After a small dip in the road my stomach growled. The music in my head was pushed aside by the delicious aroma wafting to the front of the car. A warm loaf of wheat bread lay nestled near my cello on the back seat. My mother took it out of the oven minutes before we left the house, and when I placed it in the car its yeasty crust, full and round, spilled over the edges. I licked my salty fingers as butter shimmered down the sides and settled deep into the metal loaf pan. Before settling into my seat, I covered it with a dishtowel.

My mother drove our small black Volkswagen Beetle up our gravel lane. There had been an April downpour days earlier and potholes lay hidden under muddy water. Her face drew tight as she whipped the wheel to avoid the deep ones. At the top of the lane, we stopped. Morning fog rolled past before we turned onto the highway. I took a quick glance to the back seat to check my cello in its brown canvas case. Threadbare with loose stitching in spots, the cello inside was ready. I was not.

The cold vinyl passenger seat cut through my Sears corduroy pants and I pulled my sweatshirt sleeves over my hands, wrapping my fingertips tight within my palms. Warm fingers were crucial if I had any hope of success. Between my feet sat a bit of relief from the chill. A glass gallon jar of white frothy milk rested on the floor clenched between my Hush Puppy shoes. Fresh that morning from Betsy, our Guernsey cow, it warmed my lower legs. A piece of Cut-Rite wax paper placed under the lid kept the milk from escaping.

I shivered. A small cloud of my breath hovered in front of me. I took no notice of fruit trees in bloom or fields of sprouting hay. With only one hour to learn my lesson music, I closed my eyes and fingered the assigned etudes and scales on my forearm. In a house with nine others, plus farm chores and homework, eking out practice time was a chore in itself. My lesson loomed, sending another shiver through my thin frame. I hadn't practiced. All week.

My fingers slowed as my mind wandered to Science class. Last week we studied osmosis. Could it or some undiscovered scientific phenomenon transfer the fingerings and bowings from my fingers through my arm and up to my brain? I took a couple shallow breaths. I should have put the manuscript under my pillow last night. But now with little hope, I bit my lip harder and increased the speed of my drumming. Somehow the movement of notes and rhythms eased my nerves.

Arriving at my teacher's house the still warm milk and bread were placed gingerly on his dining room table. I unpacked my cello in his music room and sat down. My fingers were cold, but heat rose from inside my sweatshirt as Mr. Wendt bent over and adjusted the height of the music stand. Leaning forward, his full round belly held in by a crisp white shirt, bulged over a black belt and touched his knees.

"Let's start with your scale," he said.

I stumbled up and down the two octave G major scale—the one with the shift to fourth position—and he clicked his tongue. My face grew hot. I floundered through my etude, missing flats and accidentals. My throat felt like I had swallowed barbed wire and I held in a cough.

The silence of the room broke when he said, "How's your solo?"

My bow hand was moist with nervous sweat, and I wiped it on my corduroy pants. The ridges of the fabric moved to and fro under my palm. Anything to delay the first movement of my

Romberg Sonata. Missed fingerings, backward bowings and incorrect rhythms flew past me—*allegro non troppo; fast, but not too fast*. At the end of the dismal performance, my chest was tight from holding my breath. My teacher asked no questions, made no comments, and I released my breath—*poco a poco; little by little*. I looked straight ahead but heard his heavy sigh. My cheeks burned.

Mr. Wendt picked up his full size cello to demonstrate a particular phrase, and I was glad to hide behind my smaller instrument. He played the melody full of vibrato, dynamics, and emotion. The phrase soared and I glanced through the doorway into his dining room. On the cloth covered table rested the buttery bread next to an abandoned coffee cup. I squinted to the back of the house where a sunroom held a bank of low windows. The sun's rays wrapped around my mother's head like the halos of saints that stood in St. Anne's Catholic church.

Bent over an ironing board, steam rose to her face as she pushed the hot iron back and forth over one of my teacher's white shirts. Tiny wisps of hair had escaped the bun at the top of her head and lay limp against her brow and cheeks. Her forehead glistened.

Her tired eyes met mine.

The following day I practiced, and the day after that, and the day after that.

THE PARENTS
By Pam Tucker

What happened to the possessive,
the endearing "my" that held us
hand in hand, a band of three?

Having dinner with the parents.
Be done in twenty—
his text sounding like a sentence:

twenty years hard labor
of silverware and small talk
over a plate of sirloin tips.

Our son, bright possessive
of our making, chats, smiles,
his night soon spooling free without us,

and though the room rings
with talk and laughter, waiters
sweeping through with water, bread,

we, *the parents,* seem left
to speak through the tinny mic,
the wall of Plexiglas, visiting

hour nearly over. We press our palms
to the wall through which we see
and hear, but can no longer seem to touch.

ELUSIVE APOLOGY
By Mary Krakow

Was it spite, or blind insensitivity? Either way, the oak Dad trained to the fence between lawn and carport is gone. It was his lasting legacy, a living testament to his love of all things botanical. I can't say for certain how long the espalier graced the yard, but Dad's been gone twenty-three years. It had been the backdrop of lawn parties and family photos for decades.

How do I forgive her?

I told her I was sad the tree Dad trained to the fence was gone. Instead of apologizing for having it cut down, she insisted it was damaging the fence. The trunk had indeed grown around the chain wire mesh supporting the espalier. The fence was doing its job.

What if I don't forgive her?

She seems oblivious to the pain she caused by its removal. She implies she's done a favor, a good deed. She has no need of my forgiveness. In her eyes she did no wrong.

Why forgive her?

Dad's oak will never recover. It is gone. Dad is gone. Forgiveness is my only salvation.

19 CANDLES: LIVING WITH FIRE
By Jennifer Delahunty

On the day I moved back to Central Oregon eight summers ago, I counted the ponderosas in my new front yard: nineteen. Close to my house. On that July moving day, the sky had an otherworldly glow, and I could taste the air—acrid, smoke soaked. I had been gone from Central Oregon for a dozen years, and neither the bitter smell of the air nor the blood-orange sky registered as familiar. I had lived in this forest-rich place in the late 90s, but fire's smell and sky were new to me.

For my second move to Central Oregon, I chose to live in Sisters, an old logging town which has been devastated by fire twice. California's 2018 Paradise Fire got our attention—Paradise was a picturesque mountain town, just like ours. Still, the idea of our little village going up in smoke sounded like an abstraction, something not likely to happen, right?

Or so we hope. But evidence accumulates.

On Labor Day 2020, my family and I had been scheduled to go to the Opal Creek Forest Center off Santiam Pass and stay in a rustic cabin sheltered by old-growth Douglas firs. An email from the center stated there was a "small fire," about 400 acres, up the valley, but it was "under control." Still, they said, they would need to cancel our visit out of caution. No amount of caution was enough to keep this very same place from burning to the ground within days of that email. But I get ahead of my story.

With our long weekend plans cancelled, we cobbled together a backyard picnic instead. The sunflowers in the vase on the table were from my garden. Halfway through lunch, they quivered slightly, then threatened to tip over. The wind was picking up, shifting, blowing from the east. The east? That hardly ever happens. We looked up and watched the white clouds overhead flow in an uncommon direction. Our napkins flew off the table.

As the winds quickly grew to forty, then fifty, miles per hour, the Beachie Creek fire—the "small fire" that cancelled our holiday plans—bloomed and moved west. My daughter left the picnic and drove back over the Santiam Pass to her home in Portland. We weren't worried—yet. Just south of the Opal Creek Forest Center where we would have been staying, she shot a video through her windshield. It was shocking: an entirely crimson sky, pulsing like neon. Minutes later, officials closed the road, and the conflagration came through like a high-speed train, destroying homes, melting vehicles, and killing people. The tires on my daughter's car had to have been hot. Suburbs close to Portland prepared to evacuate.

Over the next couple of weeks, three major fires totaling 400,000 acres consumed a large swath of the Willamette and Jefferson National Forests, including the Opal Creek Ancient Forest Center. These fires burned until the snow fell in late October.

Had the winds blown that Labor Day from west to east, as they normally do, my house and the entire town of Sisters would have been, most likely, toast.

This is the mathematics of fire in the American West: spark + wind = inferno.

Ironically, the eastern side of the Cascade Mountains, this parched and fire-ripe area, is booming like so much of the West. Just down the road from me, the city of Bend now appears on *USA Today* maps, having busted through 100,000 in population. In recent years, the whole area has gone wild—houses being bought by cashed-out Californians for a hundred thousand dollars over asking, the new owners not even flushing the toilets before plunking down their dough. Since the pandemic began, Bend has been declared both a boom town and a "Zoom town" by national news sources.

Bend is aptly named as it has twisted and morphed since being founded in the early 1900s. After the lumber boom went bust in the 1970s, Bend civic leaders installed a bronze statue on a downtown street of a man sitting on a park bench, leaning on his thighs, opening his wallet. This little town suffered mightily for several decades—until tourism moved in. An extinct volcano, Mt. Bachelor, became a popular ski resort. Golf courses, mountain biking trails and zip lines followed. Today, Lamborghinis circle the parking lots of the private schools in town.

Changes in this part of Central Oregon are emblematic of what is happening across the entire Western United States. So much money, not enough rain, the affluent masses seeking a slice of natural beauty, erecting their slant-roofed, 3,000 square-foot, energy-efficient homes to frame a view of the jutting mountains. I live in a small, low-ceilinged cabin from the late 70s with no air conditioning or mountain views and that cluster of ponderosas in my front yard—my nineteen tapers, tall torches that remain unlit. For the moment.

Why live here? It's a fair question, but I don't have to dig deep for answers: The intoxicating whiff of juniper after a rain. The brazenness of the winter sun. Urgent mountain streams of snow melt. Chantarelles poking through the volcanic duff of a September forest floor.

Quite simply, I live here because it's where I feel most at home in the world.

***

The summer after the Beachie Creek fire, I was visiting my sisters, all of whom stayed put in the Midwest. Minnesota was awash in vibrant green, though it too had had lower than average rainfall. I found the deciduousness intoxicating.

On a cool June morning, I received a text, then several calls, from neighbors. "There's a fire near your house," my friend said. "I'm bringing over a trailer. Make a list, and we'll take your stuff off the property." This friend had done the same thing twice for her parents when they lived in Black Butte Ranch, a development not far from mine. Her parents had evacuated their property twice in 30 years—that was the previous generation's experience of fire threat. This was the second summer out of seven where nearby fires had me zipping my "go bag."

After the call, I sat on the back steps of my sister's home and pecked my list of keepsakes out on my phone: a blanket chest my grandfather had made for my mother, my children's art work, boxes of photos and old letters. Would it be saccharine to say tears slipped down my cheeks as I pushed "send?"

While I was more than fifteen hundred miles away, my helpful friends hauled my things out of my house and drove the trailer off site. About 100 houses a mile from mine were in full-on evacuation, the residents sleeping in the school gym. My neighborhood was next to be vacated. Our generous governor opened the funding spigot and got 800 firefighters on the ground immediately; they contained the fire within the week. "She couldn't afford to lose that many fellow democrats," joked one neighbor.

When I returned home from my Midwestern vacation, my friend asked, "Why don't we just leave everything you care about in the trailer for the rest of the summer?"

Is this what life has come to in the West?

As climate change moves front and center and our past forest practices prove their failure, Central Oregon has gone from timberland to tinderland. Is it inevitable that my front yard candles *will* burn? If so, do I leave now before fire takes it all? Or is the risk of living here until then worth the rewards? And then I ask the unutterable question: Am I on the brink of becoming a climate vagabond, just like millions across the globe?

I feel a bit like the bronzed man on the park bench in downtown Bend, opening not my wallet, but my heart, to see if I have enough love and courage to remain in Central Oregon.

WINDBREAKERS
By Pam Tucker

In spring kids molt
long johns, parkas,
fur-lined boots,

slip into new skin

windbreakers
    light as kite paper.

They flutter to school
like pastel flags

sidestepping
gravel-pocked drifts
dripping with melt—

    the world sloughing
    its winter wear.

Like a toothless cur,
wind nips and bristles,
all bluster now,

flaps sleeve-wings
outstretched
as kids fly uphill
toward home,

the final school bell
scattering kites
into a germinal
summer sky.

CHILDHOOD REMEMBERED
By MJ Kuhar

The abandoned park was slowly being taking over by the forest. While driving through the Western Pennsylvania hills in late June on route to his home in Philadelphia, something compelled JR to stop and visit what remained of *Storybook Forest*, one of his favorite childhood haunts. It was his fiftieth birthday and he was feeling nostalgic. He remembered being five years old when he visited for the first time: seeing Humpty Dumpty teetering on the wall; the sticky feel of cotton candy on his fingers; and talking to Red Riding Hood. He'd come back every summer with his twin sister on their birthday until, at the ripe old age of nine, he'd declared he was too old for make believe.

JR pushed his way through the wild rose brambles and Queen Anne's lace on the overgrown path. In the distance, he took in the tall mast of the once gallant pirate ship in its dried-up lake, the crooked man's derelict house, and the oversized crumbling beanstalk. He remembered meeting a jolly pirate on that ship who'd given out peppermint candies, and a scary giant next to the beanstalk, who he later realized was a normal sized man walking on stilts. Red Riding Hood stood outside Granny's house and carried a basket with individually wrapped shortbread cookies to share with hungry parents and kids. His sister had been fascinated by Red and asked her to push down her hood so she could see her hair.

Rounding a bend, JR spied the Old Lady's Shoe and was jarred from his reveries. It had a fresh coat of paint, some red and white petunias in pots along the walk, and a small fountain gurgling beside the front door. A gabled window stood ajar with a white ruffled curtain swaying in the breeze. When he closed his eyes, he imagined he heard children's happy voices giggling and shouting.

Ambling toward The Shoe for a closer look, JR savored the early morning freshness of the summer day as the sun peaked over the trees. Approaching The Shoe, he decided it looked like an oddly shaped tiny house. He fantasized about who might live there. A shiny metal slide protruded from the side, and he chuckled as he recalled racing his sister up the interior stairs to see who could get to the top and slide down first.

Gazing off into the dense woods, JR conjured a long-forgotten image of his sister as a carefree child and then again as a sullen teen. He hadn't seen her since she'd run away from home on their sixteenth birthday.

Walking up the cobbled path of the well-kept tiny shoe-house, JR was sure he heard voices and laughter. The door opened, and several small children appeared. Although he was clearly visible on the deserted path, the children skipped right past him. He thought it quite odd no one seemed to notice him until one impish girl detached herself from the others, waved excitedly, and smiled. "JR, you came! You remembered."

**

A state police cruiser, light bar flashing, marked the site of a single vehicle accident along the busy highway next to the shuttered entrance of *Storybook Forest*. The ambulance hadn't yet arrived. The trooper shook his head sadly at the sight of a red BMW convertible wrapped around a tree next to the faded book-shaped sign. The middle-aged male driver was clearly dead. A second trooper pulled up, slammed the cruiser into park and jumped out.

He and the first trooper approached the BMW and leaned inside. As they wrenched open the passenger door, a leather wallet fell onto the crushed weedy growth. The first trooper studied the driver's license and noted it was the man's birthday.

"Poor sap," he said. "Bad luck dying on your birthday." He looked at the cloudless blue sky. "Wonder what happened. Weather doesn't seem to be an issue."

"Maybe he had some kind of medical condition," the other man replied.

The first trooper handed over the wallet as he inspected the car's interior. "See if you can find any info about next of kin."

Rooting through the wallet's pockets, the second trooper pulled out an old black and white photo of two grinning children standing next to a man dressed like a pirate.

"Looks like maybe it was taken at this park, you know, back in the day."

The first trooper straightened up, an odd look on his face. "Funny thing," he commented as goose bumps appeared on his arms and he shivered in spite of the warm day. "This is the seventh accident in this exact same location since the park closed a decade ago."

BUDDHA WITH ONE EAR:
BECOMING AN OLD WOMAN
By Barbara Cole

Today I became an old woman. Seventy-five to be specific. Holy flipping wrinkled and crinkled alligator and crocodile skin years. How could that be?

I'm still nine years old, bossing my mother around as I prepare for my first slumber party. I'm eleven, concluding that nothing is more important in life than to be happy. To be successful, one needs to learn how to be popular. I read, I take myself to charm school, join or start numerous clubs, and learn exercises to keep my waist small and be personable. I'm nineteen when I agree to marry my husband the night I return from my mother's funeral.

Thirty-five when I finish my doctorate, embarrassed I'm so old. Forty when I buy enough land to graze cows, corral horses, and raise 499 chickens. Forty-seven when I fall in love for the nth time, only to be rejected for the nth plus time. Fifty-something when I close my company's doors and start traveling internationally, teaching management and loving developing countries.

Sixty when close friends and I enjoy tickets to favorite comedian Jay Leno's show in LA. Later I sneak off alone to Baja where chickens under the table and enchiladas atop the table give me unexplained joy as I look over the Pacific. New York City, sometime in those years are where two close friends and I celebrated. Today I wear the Chinese bracelet one gave me for that occasion.

I have been busy during all those years. Raising kids, you say? Nope, not me. I was fortunate to have a mother tell me the worst thing that could happen to a woman was to be pregnant.

I made pretty sure that wasn't going to happen. Plus, I changed enough diapers as a children's hospital nurse aide and I don't like shrill little people's screams, cute as their faces and innocent as their souls may be.

What have I been doing all these decades?

I was busy trying to keep myself afloat financially, to live life. Most of the time I was successful, at least, sufficiently so to keep the wolves away. Staying afloat is different from breathlessly swimming long laps. I never could have competed with the female Michael Phelps equivalent in swimming or financially.

So here I sit. Seventy-five years behind me. A lot fewer ahead of me if observation is to be believed. What regrets do I have?

I don't know if these are regrets or wishes. I wish I had accumulated more money. I wish I had some real accomplishments under my belt, ones that made true differences in many, many people's lives. Yes, I did affect some folk positively, but I wish I could have made more of an impact. Developed an impressive vaccine. Sent eighty-six orphaned kids through college. Found ways for warring tribes to work together in peace.

Financial or education success were not my only goals. Not dying early from boredom was another. Some are able to stay with the same partner, in the same house, in the same job for decades. I, on the other hand, when I was four was pretty sure I would meet all the people in the world.

Some day.

Discovering what was around the next corner, how to start a hedge fund, create a Grand Marnier souffle or sail alone around the world were things I wanted to know.

Maybe it would be enjoyable to have some adult children who would care for me. Perhaps but no, not much regret there. Too many adults are unhappy with their children and the children either despise their parents or they remain in their care, even producing offspring which the parents must now manage.

I'm on my own.

Always have been. Always will be, even though I'm involved in a relationship.

What do old women do?

That depends on who the old women are. Some of them were old at forty-five, choosing to do little besides sit, drink, crochet, gossip. Others at 102 are doing downward dogs, running marathons, and a host of other activities in which they find joy.

Joy. That's seems to be the key to much in life. Doing what you want to do, when, how, where, and with whom, or no one.

A better question might be what does this specific old woman do? That's me.

Some have told me that I have lived my life my way. Perhaps I have to some small degree. If so, I will put that on my "I'm proud of . . . " list. Maybe what pulls me back from that is what I haven't had the courage or ability to do. Maybe it was energy I lacked even as I'm usually rated above many others in energy levels. What happened? Maybe I just wore out. Maybe, maybe, maybe.

I sit here today, alone, at my self-imposed retreat. A few people have emailed to wish me a happy birthday. Five years ago, I had the most wonderful birthday party anyone could have, surrounded by friends saying all kinds of complimentary statements about me. One of those attending has moved on to his next life, far from what seemed the time for him to go.

I've spent many other birthdays alone, not by choice. Then I felt sorry for myself, eating alone in a place I didn't want to be. No one acknowledging the day. Today's aloneness is by choice. I have wanted little more than peace, quiet, no one I know near me except my thoughts. At an old resort in central Mexico, I did a silent meditation around the property, admiring white irises, a towering star palm with a cactus growing out of its side twenty feet in the air, and myriad other flowering and green plants. A woodpecker pecked at the palm next to it and a hummingbird flitted below while I admired the Nochebuena, or poinsettias as English-speakers know them, blooming long after the Christmas holidays have gone.

Walking around one corner, breathing in, breathing out, I spied a large wooden Buddha, looking comfortable and familiar, with one ear falling. I could relate. Maybe one of my ears is falling, making me less likely to hear what I need to hear in life, even to see what I need to see for my remaining years. Thankfully, both my hearing and seeing are in perfect order, yet I wonder. As more years are added to my chronological line, will I become more like the old wooden structure, sitting there, watching life go by as I disintegrate into the earth?

We expect a lot out of life, or at least those of us who have had the good fortune to live privileged lives, do. Even if we have started life with demographics that would not announce our future successes to the world, as we acquire more physical economic goods we expect things to be different in a positive way. We expect to have a beautiful house, participate in an amicable relationship. We expect others to treat us kindly, with respect, even dignity. We expect, we expect . . .

Yet life isn't like that for all of us.

Abraham Hicks tells us "The reason you want every single thing that you want is because you think you will feel really good when you are there. But, if you don't feel really good on your way to there, you can't get there. You have to be satisfied with what is while you're reaching for more."

Be satisfied? But that's not what many self-help gurus and others have told us through the years. We should want more, we should do more, we should be more. We should, should, should. And yes, I guess the world can get to be a better place when Robert Moses builds expressways all over NYC and activists protest those same expressways which have torn apart communities. Groups on both sides had the opportunity to display their best efforts toward what they believed should be done. When their life is done, some of them have and will feel they fulfilled their purpose in this lifetime.

You have to be satisfied . . . Abraham, the entities who appear to have lived zillions of years ago and now communicate their wisdom via channeling through Esther Hicks, say. Even if you don't like Hicks or you don't believe in ageless entities providing guidance for your life, you have to admit the advice is not all bad. Isn't it easier to be satisfied with what you are reaching for, all the while expecting more? Wait a minute. Isn't that contradictory?

But much of life is contradictory.

So, who you gonna blame? Buddha with his ear falling off? Some incomprehensible entity? Yourself? You can do any of these, but the blame won't get you a year older or younger.

Written by a now officially old woman.

SHALLOWS
By Kathryn Mattingly

Who only sails
calm seas, free
from waves of
pain, never to be
washed ashore
in grief's clutch?

Only those who
have not tasted
the salty sea on
another's lips,
or longed for
love's bounty.

Who doesn't
plunge beneath
the surface of
their fears, where
a barren life waits
to be fulfilled?

Only those who
coast the shallows
of repressed desire,
not letting anyone
past the barriers
of their heart.

It's a tragic voyage
smooth as glass,
with nary a wind
to test the sails for
strength, endurance,
or vulnerability.

A GIFT FOR EULA
By Mary Krakow

Eula sat by the parlor window, watching and waiting. She tugged at the stiff starched collar on her Sunday dress. The lace scratched her neck. Sleeves hung to her wrists where she had dabbed Mother's perfume. Her hem skimmed the top of brown button boots. Two ribbons the color of freshly churned butter held her unruly hair from her shiny scrubbed face. Dark tresses settled in lazy rivers down her back.

The wick on the kerosene lamp had been trimmed awaiting Dad's return. Mother said he'd come on the afternoon train. Eula went to the window right after breakfast, just in case. She peered into the lane in front of Grandmother's home. When Dad shipped his ponies to the East, Eula and her mother always stayed with her. Their ranch was no place for a woman alone with a small child, he said. Grandmother's home was on top of a hill near town not far from the railroad tracks.

At Grandmother's, Eula visited with cousins, helped with chores, and attended church. She enjoyed her trips to civilization but having Dad home meant she could return to carefree life on the ranch. Now that she was seven, she roamed barefoot from ranch house to creek and corral. How she loved to climb onto the wide fence slats and talk to the ponies. Their horsy scent clogged her nose.

Mother called from the kitchen. "Eula, lunch time."

"I want to stay here." She pouted.

"The train isn't due for another hour."

She left her post at the window. Mother retied her sagging hair ribbons. Sitting and waiting was hard work. After lunch Eula excused herself and returned to the parlor. She leaned back into the settee and drifted off.

In her dream, the wind moaned E. . .u. . .l. . .a. She blinked her eyes open and realized the train had arrived!

Mother joined her in the parlor. Eula was unable to sit a moment more. She bounced from the settee to the window. Pent up energy set her feet dancing. Soon the clop clop of horse's hooves on the lane pounded in her chest. She rushed to the door and ran onto the wide porch. Mother followed close behind. Dad leapt from the carriage and gathered them to him. Eula buried her face in his coarse traveling suit. She breathed in city smells and miles of cigar smoke. His muscular arms reunited them. Eula, Mother, and Dad were a family, together again. He kissed Mother tenderly and stroked her hair. Eula tipped her face up and was rewarded with a scratchy, bearded kiss.

Dad pressed his calloused hand against her soft cheek and whispered, "I brought my princess something from Omaha."

Eula hopped up and down with excitement.

The driver threw down Dad's satchel.

Grandmother set a tray of sweet tea and biscuits on the parlor table. Dad took a long pull from his tea, smacked his lips like a cowboy, and brushed the drips from his mustache. He reached into his satchel and pulled out the oddest thing Eula had ever seen. It looked like a cluster of giant yellow pea pods. "What is it?" she asked.

Dad began to spin his tale. "If there is a thing to be had, one can find it in Omaha. I searched for the perfect gift to bring my princess. Jewels? No, they are too common. Fine dresses? Not exotic enough. I wandered through the marketplace and followed my nose to a most unusual stand. A little brown man cried 'Fruits from the tropics, foods of the gods.' He lured me with a dripping chunk of yellow fruit." Dad smacked his lips at the memory of the pineapple. "I sampled every exotic fruit he had to offer, finally settling on the banana. It was shipped from Mexico, land of palm trees and endless summers." He broke a pod from the cluster and handed it to Eula.

She raised it to her mouth like an ear of corn. Dad stopped her.

"Skin it before you eat. Like a varmint."

He cracked the end open and pulled strips of peel until they dangled around his fist. She took the pale yellow tower from him and sunk her teeth into the soft flesh.

"Mmmmm." She squished the banana to pulp with her teeth and swallowed.

"What do you think?" Dad asked.

"I don't want to be your princess anymore."

"Why not?"

"I want to be a goddess and eat bananas every day!"

NATIVE-BORN IMMIGRANT
By Ginger Dehlinger

I exit the air-conditioned office building through a revolving door that has been trying to take a bite out of my heel for a year. The abrupt change from cool, dry lobby to sultry street is like a slap in the face.

It's 5:15. Waves of people press in on me, some from the thirty-story building I just left, others streaming along a sidewalk twice as wide as those in my home town. The first time I entered this torrent of humanity, I thought I might be swept off my feet and carried downstream like a helpless leaf. Much to my surprise, these city people maintain a hurried, yet disciplined pace—one side walking east, one west as if they all attended the same kindergarten.

I'm wearing my fawn-colored suit and an off-white blouse the shop girl called alabaster. The taupe canvas bag strapped diagonally across my chest makes me boring beige from my ash blond hair to my fake leather pumps. I wear the same colorless color Monday, Wednesday, Friday, black on Tuesdays and Thursdays. Some of the female executives I share the elevators with wear red suits or dresses, but that color appears to be reserved for higher pay grades.

I felt perfectly comfortable wearing red and other bright colors before moving here, but within a week I realized my clothes were all wrong, some items outright hokey in this fashion-focused city. Now, the clothes I brought with me hide in the back of my closet while I max out my BankAmericard in an attempt to look like I belong in the same business as the suits and Fifth Avenue fashionistas who work in my building. On my way to and from work every day, I walk alongside people wearing every manner of dress from the hottest new fashions to shredded jeans and tank tops. Some carry Gucci bags, others wear backpacks. I have even seen a few turbans and kaftans. Most of the people live or work here. Those strapped to backpacks are probably tourists.

Is that what I am? Forever a tourist? I thought I would feel like a New Yorker by now. Maybe I should pack up and return to the small farming community I left behind. Why am I still gasping for air in this sea of diversity?

It's crazy here. Last week, I saw a man decked out in chest waders and a hat bristling with lures and flies. He was holding a good-looking flyrod over an open man hole. I still have a lot to learn about this city, but I know fish don't swim in its bowels. I'm also sure the wannabee fisherman was not making a fashion statement with his fancy gear; he was one of those bona-fide New York wackos I see nearly every day, muttering on street corners or shouting at people waiting for a bus. I have seen two almost-naked guys in Times Square, one wearing briefs, one covered with a sandwich board. I don't remember what the second guy was advertising on that board covering his bare behind.

The sun won't set for hours on this sweltering August night, yet the streets are already cloaked in shadow. It's as if these asphalt canyons are walled by gigantic brick and steel fences. Not only do the multi-story buildings hide the sun, but with few gaps for wind to clear the air, it's humid as hell down here. My arm pits are beyond damp, my suit a bag of wrinkles. I could cool off some if I removed my jacket, but that would expose my clingy blouse and the stark white bra beneath it.

I spend way too much time and effort getting back and forth to work in this city. The subway station I use every day is six ridiculously long blocks from my office building, and the train ride to Queens takes half an hour. When I get off the train at

Queens Boulevard, I walk another eight blocks to my apartment, thankfully, much shorter blocks than those in Manhattan. Before moving here, all I had to do Monday through Friday was open the garage door, slide onto the seat of my Jeep, and drive four and a half miles to an office building in a strip mall.

As I hurry along the sidewalk with the rest of this evening's rush hour striders, I'm thinking how good it will feel when I step out of my heels, peel off my panty hose, open a cold beer, and plop onto the spongy sofa in my studio apartment. I spent most of this day typing sales projections for my supervisor and running errands—one to mail a package at a seedy store doubling as a post office where I was the only person in line who didn't roll up on a bicycle. I have yet to figure out why I need the college degree stipulated in the classified ad I answered, an ad that should have read: *Must be willing to schlep and grovel.* Schlep is a word I learned not long after I was hired—not from my boss—from the person who trained me. Grovel was already part of my vocabulary when I moved here. Both words describe what I do all day.

I have acquired many new words this past year, at work and at play, mostly terms and slang expressions borrowed from foreign languages. I get a kick out of slipping these words into my own conversations as long as I can use them correctly and without sounding like a phony. English is my native tongue. Most of the people I come in contact with also speak the language, though I don't always understand them due to a variety of accents, some cab drivers with accents that are indecipherable.

This new vernacular has given me a profound appreciation for how difficult it must be for foreigners, especially those who don't speak English, to move to this country. I didn't migrate across an ocean to get here, just one continent, every inch inhabited by English-speakers.

Suddenly, a man walking near me accidentally bumps me with his briefcase—a fortuitous nudge that warns me I'm approaching the mouth of the station where I catch the E train. I follow part of the crowd down a long bank of cement steps. On my way down, I am amused by how closely the drumming of a hundred shoes on concrete sounds like Canada geese flapping their wings on takeoff. I hope for coolness underground, but the temperature barely lowers as we descend into sun-starved air that smells of urine and ancient dirt.

At the turnstile, I swipe the MetroCard I have clutched in my hand since I left work. I hate being yelled at for holding up the line while I dig through my purse. I pass through the turnstile like a pro, and then head for the dimly-lit platform where I blend into a group of people two rows back from the tracks. Not much conversation takes place as we wait, absorbed in our own thoughts. The man in front of me is reading a newspaper. I can't quite make out the headlines, but if it's something important, I'll catch it tonight on the evening news.

More people gather on the platform. Hearing the crunch of paper, I look to my right and see a woman wearing a yellow kerchief pull a bagel out of a bag clutched to her chest. The oniony smell makes me hungry. All I had for lunch was an egg salad sandwich.

The woman is halfway through her bagel when the rumble of wheels signals an approaching train. Two glaring bright eyes appear on my left before the steel beast lumbers out of the tunnel. The motorman sounds the horn, and my ears suffer the shrieking of brakes until the train marked Queens Boulevard grates to a stop. A strident bell jangles. The doors open, and I am swept, along with the bagel lady, into an already crowded car. Within seconds, the bell jangles again and the doors close. I assume the car can't possibly hold another passenger when a young man in a gray suit pokes his hands between the doors' rubber liners, forces them apart, and squeezes inside.

There is never an empty seat on this train. Packed like spears of canned asparagus, we can't possibly fall on our faces, but I, wanting more stability, head for the middle of the car and one of the sturdy poles mounted to the ceiling.

"Excuse me . . . excuse me," I say, mostly to myself, as I maneuver through the crowd.

Protocol dictates standing sidelong to the pole in order to accommodate the most bodies. As the train starts to move, I wrangle a bit of space between two beefy commuters, one wearing a sleeveless blouse, one a denim work shirt. Since I'm a hair over five feet tall, I usually find an empty spot at the bottom of the pole. Blindly, I reach downward, wondering, as I do on days like this, if the bottom of the subway pole heralds my destiny.

In no time, I am dancing to the same tune as the pole people, swaying from side to side and careening around corners in sync with the rhythm of the train. No one talks much, although, to be fair, doing so would mean having to shout over the roar of the wheels. No one smiles, either. Every face wears the dreary mask of resignation I see on most subway riders this time of day.

My hand is skin to skin with the one above, but it is impossible to see through the tangle of arms and shoulders who that hand belongs to. Farther up the pole, hands are stacked like a multi-flavor ice cream cone—the same flavors I walk alongside every day, work with, eat lunch with—a far richer assortment of flavors than the vanilla world I grew up in.

We're halfway to Queens when the motorman unexpectedly brakes hard. I let out a yelp as the jolt launches me into the back of the woman in the sleeveless blouse. I tell the woman I'm sorry, but she is probably so accustomed to people bumping into her she doesn't even turn around. I am surprised the man in the denim shirt didn't slam into me. He must have a solid grip on that pole.

The train quickly regains speed, and I bounce from foot to foot to keep my balance while I reach for my spot. Back where I belong again, I relax a little, look at my watch, think about what I'm going to have for supper, and in less than a minute I feel someone pat my fingers. It felt like a pat, anyway. Did the person's hand slip off the pole the way mine did when the train lurched? Our ride has been smooth since the jolt that made me stumble. Did the man or woman who touched me nod off for a second? It's awfully stuffy in here.

I feel another pat, this time more pet than pat, more stroke than stumble. I scan the faces closest to me and see no change, not even a twinkle in someone's eye. My gut reaction is to move my hand but doing so would mean letting go of the pole.

The pets or pats or whatever they are continue, however sporadically, and since I will be getting off the train shortly, I leave my hand where it is. I do this mostly for stability, but also because pulling my hand away wouldn't be very neighborly. I don't want to add rejection, albeit a small one, to someone else's bad day. Besides, I kind of like the way it makes me feel—a bit daring, a bit crazy, maybe even crazy as a bona-fide New Yorker. I bite back a smile as I stare into the sleeveless blouse an inch from my nose.

AUTUMN'S FLEETING LOVE
By Siobhan Sullivan

the wisest ones wait
impatient trembles of green
longing for fall's kiss

scarlet embraces
gold whispers, orange laughter
autumn's fleeting love

HERSHEY
By Kathryn Mattingly

Hershey looked up from his book and watched the streetlamp outside his window come to life, giving off a warm glow. Night sounds crept in with the evening breeze. They were the same sounds as every night since he could remember . . . a city bus screeching to a halt, a truck idling at the stoplight. In the far distance an ambulance sang an eerie one-note song.

Slowly he stood to his full beanpole height of six foot four inches and headed for the kitchen. Hershey warmed his dinner with no more light than the streetlamp could offer, which was fine, since he was familiar with every nook and cranny of his three tiny rooms. While eating quietly in the near dark he heard every creak in the floorboard made by the lady above him and swoosh of the ceiling fan in the apartment below. He even felt the *thump thump thump* of the mattress when the little boy next door jumped on the bed.

Yet all of them were strangers.

Hershey had a reputation for being withdrawn, so although he received a variety of warm smiles in the rickety elevator, conversations never quite started. That was okay with him. Sometimes even the smiles were more than he could face. On those occasions he took the stairs up all three flights, thankful to be alone in the dank, dimly-lit stairwell.

Nothing unusual ever happened in Hershey's life anymore. Everything was routine and habit, as if he were simply on autopilot. Each morning at 8 a.m., he had two over-easy eggs with toast. Lunch was always precisely at noon. On even days he had roast beef and aged cheddar on sourdough. Odd days he had ham and swiss on rye. Evening meals were warmed up leftovers from Sunday, which was when he would prepare a home cooked meal. Sometimes he made his mother's ravioli from scratch, or his Uncle George's beef stew, but usually he chose a recipe from his favorite dog-eared cookbook. He would eat by the dim light of the streetlamp and then hand wash every dish, placing it carefully back in the cupboard.

After Sunday dinner, Hershey would read again in the chair by the window, barely making out the words in such scarce lighting, but on this particular night, something quite unusual happened. A foreign sound floated up from the street. Could it be laughter? Many sounds of the busy city found their way into his apartment, but never the gleeful, high-pitched laugh of a small child.

Hershey closed his book and stared straight ahead. It wasn't the faded olive wall he saw. It was a perfect April day full of tulips in every color. He recalled how the bright sun made the spring grass shimmer, while his lovely wife pushed their young daughter in a swing. He could still hear her giggles of delight; still see his wife's auburn hair dance in the breeze. The park itself was a blur of metal structures and wooden benches, but the cheery flowers, warm sunshine, and dewy grass were as clear in his mind as Charlotte's laughter, just like the laughter drifting in his window right now from the street below.

Suddenly a loud screech and the sound of metal crunching replaced the child's laughter floating on a breeze. Hershey stood abruptly and the book fell to the floor. In one giant step he was leaning out the window, watching water gush up from the fire hydrant on the curb below. A small crowd had gathered around two figures lying in the street. He was almost certain it was the single woman and little boy from the apartment next door. Steam rose from a car smashed against the bright yellow hydrant. Was he still daydreaming or had this really happened? Could they have been hit by a car? Surely, this couldn't be a repeat of what snuffed out the light from his world forever!

Hershey flew from his apartment and down the stairs two steps at a time, running through the entryway and out onto the sidewalk. Hershey was soon beside them as they lay there in a crumpled heap. The car had veered away just in time, hitting the hydrant after knocking down the boy and his mom. He stared at the little child laying on the pavement, his mind flashing to the silky blond curls of Charlotte. He took the pulse of the bronze-skinned woman beside the child and saw a lily-white woman's wrist instead. The boy began to cry. Charlotte hadn't uttered a sound. He'd raised her to his chest and had begged her to say something . . . anything.

Hershey pulled the dark-haired boy to him, rocking back and forth while the child screamed *mama* and choked on his own sobs. Hershey whispered, "She'll be fine. She'll be fine." In the corner of his eye, he saw the boy's mother stirring, sitting up. The crowd, thinking Hershey the father, kept their distance while murmuring to one another in hushed tones. Hershey saw red lights reflecting off the wet asphalt, and then stretchers. Soon there were medics rushing over. One of them gently took the little boy from Hershey. "Will they be okay?" he asked.

"Yes," the medic answered. "Their injuries don't appear to be serious."

Hershey nodded. "Thank God," he mumbled. "Thank God."

Soon the ambulance sped away and the crowd dispersed. Hershey took the elevator back to his apartment. As it inched crankily upwards he kept repeating under his breath, "They'll be okay, they'll be okay." He walked into his open door, which he hadn't closed on the way out, and slowly shut it. Hershey picked up his book from the floor. He glanced out the window just in time to see the water stop shooting up, but the streetlamp had sputtered out.

Hershey reached over and flipped a switch, flooding the tiny room in bright light. He began to read while relishing the ease of it, every word crisp and clear. He wondered why he'd never flipped the switch before, and why God takes some too soon, but spares others. He wondered if Charlotte would have liked the little dark-haired boy. He pictured them holding hands along a tulip-lined street, brown curls bouncing beside her blond ones. Most of all, Hershey wondered if the snuffed out streetlamp had lit up inside him, where there was now a warm glow.

HOPE
By MJ Kuhar

Evie and Leon Coleman entered the lobby of the McArthur Fertility Institute and stood closely together. They passed through an imposing glass door into a whole other world—one that was high tech and impersonal. The majestic building had an impressive lobby which soared upwards for two stories and boasted a melodious water feature and modern wall sculpture. On the left side of the lobby, double metal doors led to a state of the art research facility that was part of the medical school. On the opposite side, a second door, this one a deep mahogany with a discreet brass name plate, led to the outpatient fertility clinic.

Evie remembered the first time they'd passed through the impressive lobby. She'd gone over to the fountain and gazed at the glittering coins littering the bottom. Her large brown eyes had stared back at her, shimmering with so much hope. When Leon joined her, he'd fished into his pocket and handed her a shiny penny. She'd tossed it toward the far side and watched her reflection ripple in the disturbed water. Leon had smoothed her curly black hair and enveloped her in his strong arms. They'd hugged tightly, wordlessly, then joined hands and headed toward the mahogany door with the discreet name plate.

Now they'd been coming here for months in an increasingly desperate attempt to have a baby. After spending nearly their entire meager savings on one IVF cycle, they both knew if it didn't work, they would have to find another way to bring a child into their lives. The procedure two weeks ago had been technically successful, and today they would learn if the pregnancy had taken hold in Evie's womb. Standing outside the door of the clinic reception area, she drew in a breath, momentarily closed her eyes for a quick prayer, and took Leon's hand. As she reached to open the door into the hushed waiting room, he stopped her gently and whispered urgently, "Evie, I love you. No matter what."

***

Two hours later, in the small park across from the imposing McArthur Institute, autumn leaves were beginning to turn. Cheerful rust and gold chrysanthemums filled well-tended flower beds. Evie and Leon sat together on the ornamental bench, too excited to drive home. They couldn't stop smiling and whispered repeatedly, "We're pregnant! We're going to have a baby!"

"Let's go out to dinner and celebrate," Leon suggested.

"Leon, we can't. We need to save our money for the next ultrasound. Dr. Porter said we'd be able to see the heartbeat in a few weeks."

Evie absently pushed a stray curl behind her ear. "Our health insurance didn't cover any of the IVF treatment. And I'm not sure if ultrasounds during pregnancy are covered."

"Evie, you worry too much," Leon sighed, but his face revealed that he too was concerned. He worked as a mechanic, and Evie was a part time receptionist for an insurance company. Money was tight, and they hoped the pregnancy was uncomplicated so they could get ahead of their medical bills before the baby was born. As it was, they'd had to borrow money from his parents and Evie's sister.

"Maybe we'll have twins," Evie mused. "A boy and a girl."

Leon shook his head. "I just want one healthy baby," he said firmly. "That's all. And I don't care if it's a girl or a boy."

"Should we tell anyone—your parents or my sister?" Evie asked.

Leon picked up her hand in his large calloused one and kissed the palm. "Not today. Let's keep it quiet. You heard Dr. Porter. It's still really early."

"But she also said my hormone levels are excellent."

"I know, but I don't want to jinx it." Pointing to her still flat abdomen, he asked, "How do you feel? Can you tell?"

Evie slowly rubbed her lower abdomen. "Not really. I feel the same as before, a little bloated and sore." She turned to him beaming, "Oh Leon, I can't wait 'til I feel the baby move."

"But she said that's months away."

"I know. But it's all I can think about."

Leon put his arm around Evie's waist and pulled her close. "You're going to be a great mom," he declared.

"And you're going to be a great dad," she said as she hugged him back. "Now, I'm hungry. Let's go for some ice cream before we make that long drive home. Calcium is good for the baby, right?"

As they stood up, a tired looking woman pushing a massive twin stroller walked by. Inside the stroller were two sleeping infants, each wearing an identical pink hat. Evie and Leon looked at each other and grinned, "Two scoops—in a waffle cone."

***

"Are you ready, Dr. Porter?" asked Selena in her musical Jamaican accented voice. "Mr. and Mrs. Goldschmidt are in the first conference room. She's crying and he looks like he wants to punch something. I gave them some water and a box of tissues."

"I know," Joyce said. "That was how they sounded on the phone this morning. This is their third cycle, and they were so hopeful." Shaking her head slowly, she continued, "Sometimes I don't know how our patients manage to keep going. Their disappointment after a failed cycle is crushing."

Looking serious, Selena said, "Good luck Dr. Porter. I know you'll say the right thing." And with a quick wink, she added, "And I'll have an ice pack waiting in case Mr. Goldschmidt clocks you in the nose."

Joyce slowly walked down the hallway. The walls were painted a muted sage green which was supposed to help patients feel calm and comfortable. She glanced at the abstract art which vaguely reminded her of a Georgia O'Keefe painting, with its squiggling figures that looked like sperm swimming toward a vagina. It was a suitable theme, she supposed, for a fertility clinic, except here, the sperm swam in a dish and the whole act of procreation was sterile and devoid of loving intimacy.

Joyce appreciated Selena's encouragement and humor. It meant a lot that the nursing staff liked and trusted her even though she often had self-doubts. Every time one of her couples failed to conceive, Joyce felt like a failure. And lately, there had been a rash of failed cycles, and she had to wonder if there was some type of problem in the lab.

Inhaling a deep breath and mumbling a quick prayer, Joyce entered the small sunlit conference room where the couple sat at a small round table. They were professional people—he a successful financial planner, and she the part owner of a well-known event planning firm. He looked like he'd come from work, charcoal gray suit, starched white shirt and conservative red striped tie. His wife was dressed casually in black leggings, Vans slip-ons, and a mauve knit tunic top. Her wavy blond hair was pulled back in a loose ponytail, and she wore no makeup. Her eyes were puffy and red. Immediately, they both looked up.

"Hello Laura. Hello Neil. Thank you for coming," Joyce greeted them. "I know you have a lot of questions, but first let me say how sorry I am this cycle didn't work out. Please understand it's not your fault. You didn't do anything wrong. As we've discussed, there are a lot of reasons this may happen. Something might have been wrong with the embryos. Or it may be with the eggs or the sperm. Or something else. There's a lot we still don't understand."

Laura continued to weep quietly, while Neil gently rubbed her back. Several emotions flitted across his face, which finally settled into an unnatural calm. After a moment, he looked directly at Joyce and challenged, "Are you sure there hasn't been some mistake? This is our third cycle, and this is the first time there have been no embryos to transfer. The only time!"

Neil's face turned slightly red as he raised his voice. With a flash of anger and a hint of betrayal, he continued more loudly, "Maybe there's something wrong with you or your lab!"

Choosing to ignore the last comment, Joyce calmly replied, "I wish I could tell you exactly what went wrong. I've spoken with our embryologist, and he assured me all our processes are carefully monitored. He and his team are very experienced, and we have stringent quality control measures. We pride ourselves on excellent care and high pregnancy rates."

Joyce paused to give the couple time to process this news. Neil turned to his wife. "Laura," he said gently. "I'm so sorry. I know it's my fault. My sperm just aren't strong enough."

Joyce spoke quickly and reassuringly, "Neil, several of our patients have male factor infertility, and we've seen many successful pregnancies. Your sperm have successfully fertilized Laura's eggs in the past. You shouldn't assume this is your fault."

Neil's anger returned. "I just can't take it anymore! I'm a failure! I have three brothers and they all have kids. Lots of kids.

In fact, my brother Jacob said he just smiles and his wife gets pregnant." He shook his head as the anger drained away and the grief set in. "It isn't fair."

Slowly he blew out a breath and asked hesitantly. "So, what's next? Is there anything else, or does this mean we'll never have a baby?"

For the first time, Laura spoke softly, "Dr. Porter, what about donor sperm? Is that something we should try?"

Almost before she completed the sentence, Neil burst out, "Never, no way!" His eyes blazed, "Laura, we've talked about this. You know how I feel. I don't like it." Standing up so quickly that the chair crashed sideways to the floor, he raked his fingers through his short hair. Turning to face his wife, he continued angrily, "And I won't agree to it! I'd rather adopt than have some unknown college kid donor."

Absently rubbing the wedding band on her fourth finger, Laura raised tearful eyes. "And I'd like to have the joy of carrying our child and giving birth. It would still be our baby Neil. Don't you want that for us?"

Joyce took a deep breath as Laura reached for another Kleenex to dab her moist eyes and Neil righted the chair. Slowly, he sat down, his shoulders slumped dejectedly, his head in his hands.

Looking at the grieving couple, Joyce thought again about how much she hated this part of her job. This couple had already spent almost $60,000 and had nothing to show for it. Their marriage was clearly strained, and both looked like they couldn't bear much more.

The minutes dragged on as she tried to help them process their anger and grief and then move onto discussing options. When they eventually passed back through the waiting room, the other clients looked uneasily at their sorrowful expressions, and then quickly away, as if their failure to conceive might be contagious.

***

Joyce walked slowly back to her office, her hands in the pockets of her white lab coat. Although outwardly she had remained calm and professional while speaking with the Goldschmidts, she felt physically and emotionally drained. Neil's comment had really bothered her. It had been personal and accusatory. She understood his emotions—anger and grief lashing out at the only person in the room who had any power. But it still hurt. And then, it was odd that his remark had mirrored her own thoughts. What if there was something wrong in the lab? How would she even know?

Selena saw Joyce and moved towards her. "Are you OK?" she asked with concern. Pointing to Joyce's unmarred face, she joked, "It doesn't look like you need an ice pack. Maybe some chocolate?" Joyce tried to smile.

"I'm OK. But that was rough. Laura is devastated and Neil is angry because he feels so helpless, like it's his fault. They're going to take a few months off, and I suggested they see our counselor."

"Are you ready for your next patient, or do you need a few minutes? Selena asked. "They're in Consult Room 2. It's a new couple, the Millers, and they came all the way from Cedar Rapids Iowa. Have you ever been to Iowa? I hear they have a great State Fair."

"You know, I think I do need a few minutes. Are there any cookies left?"

"No chocolate chip—but we do have those peanut butter ones with the chocolate kiss on top. Take your time honey. The

Millers have family in the area who told them about McArthur. They've already been to one other IVF clinic for a consult, and they have LOTS of questions. Maybe you should have two cookies—and there's fresh coffee too. I just made a pot."

Joyce slipped into the staff lounge and poured a cup of coffee into her favorite blue mug. Selena's coffee, thick and dark, was almost like espresso. Sitting at a small table, she sipped the rejuvenating beverage while munching on a cookie and aimlessly flipping through a magazine. Five minutes later, Selena entered the room.

"I'm almost ready," Joyce said. "I reviewed their history this weekend, and it looks like their evaluation is complete. IVF is the next step for them. Did you give them our brochure and the protocol handout?"

"Just the brochure. The handout is in the folder on the desk. They're nice folks. You'll like them."

After Selena's strong coffee and the rich cookie, Joyce felt ready to continue. She quietly rapped on the door of Consult Room 2 before opening it and stepping inside. The room was almost identical to the one where she'd just met with the Goldschmidts, furnished with a small desk neatly stacked with patient education materials, a round conference table and chairs, and a potted fern.

Joyce glanced through the partially open blinds and saw the sun dappled park opposite the Institute. A woman with a double baby stroller walked slowly along the path toward a couple huddled on a bench. In the afternoon light, she saw the Millers seated at the table, just as the Goldschmidts had been. They looked at her, just as the Goldschmidts had. But the atmosphere felt very different. This room was filled with hope and possibility, not anger and despair.

Joyce acknowledged the emotional roller coaster that was her job and felt humbled by the trust of her patients. And she knew she would do her best every day to offer hope and keep that trust. She smiled as she looked into their expectant eyes and extended her hand in greeting.

"Good afternoon. I'm Dr. Joyce Porter. Welcome to McArthur Institute. How can we help you?"

SILENT ECHOES
By David Cook

Our time on earth is short
Before this land we do depart.
What mark do we leave, footprint make
On the minds and hearts of those
    Whose daily lives we invade?

No matter what we do or not,
Few at most, and most none at all,
Will remember or know of our
Short sojourn on this orb.

Yet, we are comforted to know or not,
    That even the slightest smile or nod,
Helping hand, clenched fist, or scowl
Will leave its unknown but ever felt mark
On the spirit of another human soul
And on human history forever, forever.

IT'S ALL RELATIVE
By Lynda Sather

Knowing the importance of always hiking with a buddy, I called around last month to find one. Jennifer was alphabetizing her spices. Becka had to take her gerbil to the groomers. Mary was meeting with her AA group at MacDuffy's Tavern—"Agoraphobics Anonymous," she hastened to add.

Then I remembered a gal named Suzi I'd met last February at Becka's Cinco de Mayo party. Over sushi and crepes, she'd said she was tired of ballet and would like to try hiking. I scribbled her phone number on an old bookmark stuck between pages twenty-three and twenty-four of "War and Peace." I'd taken my old college copy to the party in case Becka's brainy friend Peter showed up or I got bored. He didn't and I did, but Becka's cheap wine proved a better antidote for both than Tolstoy.

Suzi leaped at the chance to take a hike.

For our first excursion, I took her to the top of Old Baldy. "What a view!" I called down from the summit. "You can see for miles." With my encouragement, she clawed her way to the top. Unfortunately, she couldn't enjoy the vista for long as it would soon be too dark to find our way down. On the way home, we stopped to buy hiking poles and an ace bandage.

Mindful of her tired legs, I shortened our next hike by going directly down the dry wash canyon instead of walking the long way around. Faced with several unexpectedly steep drops, I showed her how to slide down the rocks on her butt. We completed the hike in record time but to the detriment of her old, and I must say, rather flimsy shorts. She emerged from our foray in one piece but her shorts looked like the tattered remains of a regimental flag after the Charge of the Light Brigade. She now wears shorts designed for Army Rangers crossing the Sahara.

Suzi had been thrilled with last week's hike in the hills towering over town. The trail was only five miles long not counting the extra mile or so it took to find the car. I told Suzi someone must have taken it for a joy ride while we were gone and left it on a different street. When we finally located the car, it was as hot as a crematory oven inside.

"I keep forgetting to get the air-conditioner fixed," I said as Suzi fiddled in vain with the knobs. "But never mind. People pay good money to take a sauna at the gym. This one's free."

Suzi mopped her brow, unrolled the window, and guzzled the last of the warm water in the gallon jug she now carried after fainting from dehydration on our first hike.

I didn't want Suzi to feel our hikes were getting too strenuous or too expensive. So, I planned today's hike along a mellow zigzag trail down a dry creek bed, the kind of creek that when you skipped a rock, dust puffed out. Unless it rained in the hills. Luckily, this was the desert.

I picked Suzi up in the new rental car the garage had loaned me when I took my old car there to get the air-conditioner fixed. Naturally, they found a few other things they insisted needed replacement—something about an alternator belt and worn-out brakes. Which is exactly the same reason I don't go to doctors anymore, not since I went to the clinic for a stomach ache and came home two days later with a whooping big hospital bill and no appendix. *If it ain't broke, don't fix it* is my motto.

Suzi and I drove down the highway singing along to the rock and roll blaring from the radio. Well, I was singing. Suzi kept turning the volume louder and louder as though to drown out my voice. When we lost the radio signal, we both fell silent, Suzi keeping one eye on Google Maps and the other on the clouds unexpectedly gathering ahead.

"I don't suppose those tennis shoes are waterproof?" I asked nonchalantly. "No? Well, never mind. You wouldn't want to break in new hiking boots while those blisters are still healing." I tried, whenever possible, to share my outdoors wisdom with her. After all, I had spent seventeen weeks, and three days in Girl Scouts—mostly making paper mâché place mats and lanyards, true. But I did earn the Outdoors Badge after camping all night, well, part of a night, in the leader's backyard. I know it was really late, like past midnight, when we all piled into her living room to watch the last half of the Johnny Carson show.

"The turnoff should be around here somewhere. Yep, here it is." I braked hard and turned onto a dirt road. The semitruck behind swerved to pass, horn blaring. "I don't know why he's so pissy," I said, giving him the finger. "There was plenty of room for the oncoming car to pass on the shoulder."

Suzi released her death grip on the armrest and retrieved her phone from the floor. "I thought you weren't supposed to take the rental car on dirt roads."

"Oh, a quick run through the car wash and they'll never know," I replied airily as the car bounced over the dirt road and only occasionally bottomed out a larger rock that couldn't be avoided.

"Shouldn't you slow down?" Suzi asked nervously. "What happens if a rock punctures the radiator?"

"It's better to drive fast and skim over the surface," I replied with assurance.

"But you've been here before?" she asked.

"Sure. Last year with Becka. It took forever to get to the trailhead the way she drove."

"How is she?" Suzi asked but not like she really cared.

"Haven't seen her in a while," I shrugged. "As soon as I mentioned hiking, she said she was scrubbing the shower grout. With a toothpick. So anal."

The day was cooler than expected, which I told Suzi was a good thing as she wouldn't have to worry about getting heat stroke like before. Still, she kept casting envious glances at my heavy hiking pants with legs that could be zipped off when the day warmed up. Even with the car's heater blasting, she had goose bumps on her bare legs.

"You said it'd be in the seventies today," she commented. "I'm freezing."

I glanced at the newfangled dashboard. "It's already sixty-eight."

"That's the heater," she said dryly.

"Never mind. You'll warm up once we start hiking."

To take her mind off the smattering of raindrops on the windshield, I asked her to check the temperature in Fairbanks, Alaska, my home town.

She tapped a few keys between bumps. "It's only twenty-seven degrees! They must be freezing."

"Twenty-seven degrees? That's a heat wave up there for February."

"Brrr!" she gave an exaggerated shiver. Or maybe it wasn't exaggerated. Goose bumps ran up and down her arms like ants at a picnic.

"Wait a minute," I said. "Is that twenty-seven degrees *above* zero?"

"What else would it be?"

"Check again."

"Oh. My. God. There's a little dash before the number."

"Twenty-seven below," I observed with satisfaction. "Now, that's cold."

I parked at the trailhead and we got out of the car. "This wind will blow the rain clouds away in no time," I assured Suzi who looked longingly back at the car. "Here, you can borrow the poncho I always carry."

As she struggled to get the flapping plastic around her, it was all I could do to keep from laughing. She looked like a wet pigeon struggling for traction in a headwind.

"That'll keep you warmer," I said, hoping to sooth her ruffled feathers.

She limped ahead of me, her trekking poles stabbing the puddles as though hoping to spear an unwary fish trapped inside.

"Wanna do the Bump and Grind trail next week?" I asked when I caught up.

"Sorry," Suzi said. "I need to schedule a root canal."

BUTTER TEA
By Niki Rainwater

Dolma and Dawa's house looks as all Sherpa houses have for the last 200 years. Free of such trappings as plumbing and electricity, the family's two-story dwelling is situated among the Himalayas, a few thousand feet above the River Solu.

Should passersby linger but a minute outside the front door, they are invited inside to refresh themselves. Dolma and Dawa have ten children to feed from their crops, and yet they generously offer boiled potatoes and butter tea; uniquely warming on a wholly cellular level.

I arrive on horseback in the late afternoon, having intermittently lost lunch, breakfast, and most of last night's dinner throughout the long ascent.

"Namaste Didi," I say to Dolma, my sister-in-law, before dismounting in a heap. A niece and nephew run to my rescue. "You're pregnant," Dolma says, cupping my face in her leathery palms. "No way," I say, Dolma smiles and I notice a few more of her teeth are missing.

My three-year old son's face appears in the window, like a ray of sunshine. "Mama!"

He has arrived ahead of us, thanks to the eldest nephew. My mother and husband round out our party. Wedding festivities have brought us here and already the house is bustling with preparations. The Tibetan calendar has dictated each detail, down to the hour of the marriage ceremony.

The hearth is a pulsating heart. Home. Coals from last night's fire are gently blown to life. One coal sparks, then another; kindling is added. Bigger hunks follow. The water kettle is placed over the open flame. Food is prepared. The added coals grow and brighten with color; pots are filled and efficiently placed among them.

My western eyes see this feat as nothing short of a miracle. Each cook pot transforms raw ingredients into a hot meal for sixteen, all at the same time! The hell with climbing Everest. Anyone who can make this happen multiple times daily is an undeniable badass.

Giant metal tongs are an all-powerful tool in the Sherpa kitchen, and Dolma is the "Tong Master." She can move one or two coals just slightly, either to raise the temperature of one dish or lower it for another. With a baby attached to her bosom. Badass.

When the noise level in the room reaches a deafening crescendo, Dolma lifts her tongs from hearth stone and gives them a swift, sharp CLACK CLACK. The room falls instantly silent. Clearly this was directed at her children, so when my mother and I snap to attention as well, Dolma seems surprised, and a little embarrassed. My admiration of her could not be greater. Two clacks, and the world is hers. Someone giggles and the whole room erupts into a cacophony of side-splitting hysterics, Dolma included.

Within minutes we resume our assigned tasks and the hum of family life again fills the room, but with a slightly lower decibel level than before. The air is thick with a love that is tangible, warming my soul like butter tea.

SAFE AT LAST
By Ginger Dehlinger

His funeral was a farce.
Who were those people in the front row
with alligator shoes
that matched their tears?

Their smarmy elegies
must have been dictated by him,
a last-ditch stab at benevolence
from a man who thought
everyone was out to get him
infect him
cheat him
cheat on him
pilfer his passwords
break down doors
and take everything he owned.

He spent a fortune on
guns
bodyguards
hidden cameras
padlocks
safe deposit boxes
Purell
N-95 masks.

He never married.
Who could he trust?

I hope he's happy, now
in his doorless, germless bunker
shielded by fescue and forget-me-nots.

FIFTEEN SECONDS
By Gerald Reponen

When I first became a young jet pilot time always seemed to drag. Most of us pilots were very impatient and expected life to be exciting and fast-moving. We were told that we were combat pilots but we were not at war. Our training missions all became very routine, not what we had expected them to be like. Then suddenly one day, reality set in. I learned what a difference just fifteen seconds could make in my life.

During 1957 and 1958 I was assigned as a combat pilot in the 30th Tactical Reconnaissance Squadron at Spangdahlem AB, Germany. My squadron was flying missions at Wheelus AFB, Tripoli in support of the missile testing program. Aircraft were there to fly high altitude visual chase missions as missiles were fired down range into the barren desert. On 19 October 1958, I was enroute to Wheelus AFB with Lt. Dick Fedosh as navigator and A/2C Bill Peterson as gunner. We were flying in the newest jet reconnaissance aircraft in the Air Force, the swept wing RB-66B.

As we passed the coast of France and started out over the Mediterranean, the right engine suddenly lost power as the fuel control went out. Declaring an emergency, I landed at the closest large airport which was Aeroport De Marseille-Marignane, France. If I had been more experienced I might have been tempted to wait until half way across the Mediterranean before declaring an emergency. I would have then recovered at an Air Force base which would have made life simpler. But being fairly new and trusted with a million dollar aircraft, I followed the advice we were told to follow, land at the nearest airport. Also, the French political situation with Algerians would have entered my mind but we knew little of the French/Algerian problems.

Upon landing we discovered Gendarmes with automatic weapons everywhere. There were many sandbagged posts around the runway and terminal area. After calling Spangdahlem Air Base and advising them on our problems, we had to catch a taxi into the city of Marseille to find a hotel. We were advised to wait for maintenance personnel to be dispatched from Spangdahlem AB, Germany to come and repair the aircraft.

On every street intersection in Marseille there were at least two armed Gendarmes with others patrolling the sidewalks. They all carried automatic weapons. We had not thought much about the Algerian terrorist problems in southern France but the Algerians had set off many explosions and vowed to destroy the airport. What an interesting situation we suddenly found ourselves in. The Gendarmes were very grim and looked at us with suspicion where ever we walked. It was quite alarming to the three of us.

It took more than a week before a maintenance crew could be flown to work on the engine. While we waited, we walked the streets and stores for something to do. I bought several different sweaters for my wife Ruth as they were different from American or German.

There was not a pneumatic starting unit on the airport so that had to be flown in to start the engines. Once the engine was repaired, I was directed to fly a test flight on the engine before I could fly the plane out of Marseille. Peterson had to repack the drag chute and install it for the next flight. A drag chute was needed to slow the aircraft down on each landing. It was very large at twenty-eight feet in diameter.

He had not attended school for repacking the large parachute but had watched the repacking of chutes at home. This would be the first actual test of his knowledge on repacking the large chute which we needed on landing to slow us down.

This being a civilian French airport, I had to call in on the radio and file a local flight plan for the test flight. We had no liquid oxygen on the aircraft and none was available. We had been told we could not fly without oxygen so I was hesitant to do so. But I was told there was no option and ordered to fly the test flight without it.

The flight was uneventful, everything worked normally. At 15,000' I shut down the engine and then restarted it. The engine continued to operate normally when power was applied so the engine test was completed. I called the tower and was advised that the runway was now closed.

In the United States a NOTAM would have been filed. This was a Notice to Airmen of any potential dangers at the airfield. Much to my surprise, Runway 32 Right, the longer runway at 7,500', had been closed while we were airborne. A trench was being dug across the runway for new electrical wiring. I had taken off with a minimum fuel load so the only option I had was to land at Marseille on the shorter runway.

Runway 32 Left was supposedly 6,000' long but seemed much shorter as there was a hill on the east approach end of the runway. We normally had to have 8,000 feet of runway for takeoff and for landing. I only had 150 hours in the RB-66 but my confidence was high even though the shorter runway worried me. The landing was firm and I immediately pulled the drag chute lever as we held our breath. The drag chute did come out eventually and with heavy braking we stopped with not much else but water in front of us. Another 100' of roll and I would have ended up in the Mediterranean Sea. I think we all sweated out the drag chute working, especially Peterson.

Two days later, the long runway was opened up again. We checked out of our hotel and got back to the airport. Checking the weather on the telephone, Spangdahlem AB, Germany was forecast to be clear at our arrival time. As a pilot flying out of a civilian airfield, I was responsible to check weather and do my own weather forecasting. I filed a flight plan and we were airborne in the early afternoon. We could not fly without oxygen and none was available. I called Spangdahlem AB and advised them of this fact again. I was then ordered to bring the aircraft home without any oxygen on board.

Without oxygen we had to fly back at 10,000' or below. Above that altitude individuals would get less than needed oxygen to function properly. The less oxygen as they rose meant the sooner they would pass out or lose their ability to function. This lower altitude took more fuel than I had calculated. As I approached Spangdahlem AB and was preparing to land, I was informed by the controllers the airfield was socked in with fog and below minimums. I was told I had to divert to my alternate airfield. The only airfield open which we could reach was Ramstein AB which had clear skies with ten miles visibility. What a relief it was to hear that information as I was starting to get quite concerned.

As we turned towards Ramstein AB which was 100 miles away, I advised the controller I was approaching 3,000 pounds of fuel and at minimum fuel. I requested an expedited landing approach. As I came up on the radio beacon for our penetration to the airfield, I was advised that the weather was deteriorating rapidly as the sun was setting. Weather was now a 300' ceiling with one mile of visibility in fog. This was the minimum conditions at which we could land the aircraft, 300' and one mile! I was now at emergency fuel with 1,000 pounds of fuel on board.

I had never landed at Ramstein AB before and did not realize that a very steep penetration was required to clear the hills. We were near the East German border and steep penetrations were required to stay clear of the East German border where we would be shot down. Approaching the airfield, I was above the steep glide path. I had the landing gear down with full flaps and the throttle near idle. There was nothing I could do to slow the aircraft down any further.

Suddenly I could see the ground below the fog as I passed the control tower, too long and too high to attempt a landing half way down the runway. I initiated a missed approach and advised the GCA (Ground Control Approach) controller I was in a dire emergency and almost out of fuel.

As I pulled up into the blackness in a tight left hand turn to downwind in the dark night fog, all of the fuel gauges were reading zero. I told my crew that at the first sign of an engine failure to eject as I would not be able to tell them with complete power loss and I would try and keep the aircraft level for them to eject.

The GCA (Ground Controllers) vectored me around in a very tight pattern at 1,000' back on to final approach. At approximately 100' above the ground and only a quarter of a mile visibility I could suddenly see the lights on the end of the runway. Traveling at over 100 knots an hour, that was just a few seconds or a brief glimpse.

I was basically on the glide slope and landing blind in the night fog. As I passed over the end of the runway lights both engines flamed out. One can just imagine what it must have been like. Traveling at over 100 miles per hour, 100 feet in the air and then closing your eyes and trying to figure out how to land the aircraft unable to see anything. I brought the nose up in the air and we touched down some place on the ground. It was complete black blinding fog where I could see nothing. All electrical went out on the aircraft. I could not see the instruments nor anything else, just total blackness. I could not talk on the radio to the crew or to the tower. Without the engines running, everything quit, a total empty feeling.

The aircraft would not glide because of the swept back wings and would have fallen like a rock. Like a bird in flight when it pulls its wings back and dives towards the ground. If the engines had flamed out just fifteen seconds earlier, we would all have died short of the runway.

I could see nothing in the blackness but somehow I managed to stay on the runway on the landing roll. Suddenly I was able to stop the aircraft not knowing where we were except we were safely on the ground, we had not died that night. Dick Fedosh was especially relieved as he had less than a month until his discharge from the Air Force and a return stateside for his pending wedding. Again, I strongly believe that God had some purpose for me later and spared my life.

When we got out of the aircraft, I found I had stopped on the runway. We could not see fifty feet in the heavy fog. Off in the distance through the night fog I could see a light glowing. We took out our bags and headed towards the light in the darkness. As luck would have it, we were heading directly towards Base Operations. We walked in and I told the airmen behind the desk I wanted to close out my flight plan. They looked startled and asked me why? I told them I had just landed my airplane and it was parked somewhere on the runway.

They said that was impossible as the airfield had been closed for the past thirty minutes in zero-zero conditions with dense fog.

Finally, we returned to Spangdahlem AB on 4 November after twenty-five days on a trip that was supposed to last one week.

I think we stopped flying missile chase missions after 1958 as I never flew to Tripoli during my tour of duty overseas.

This was just one of many stories over my career that proved how valuable every second of our life can be. I learned to appreciate every minute of my life. In this case, just fifteen seconds was the difference between life and death.

GHOSTS
By Ted Haynes

We shall hover above a scene or two, like friendly ghosts, and I will tell you happy stories, reaffirming in their way that life can be good, that people can enjoy it, that virtue and hard work are often, if not always, rewarded by days such as the one I show you now, beginning on a Saturday morning in June 2002, on a dock by Long Island Sound, where four clean-cut healthy-looking young men, college classmates a year out of school, are climbing aboard a sailboat that belongs to the father of one of them, the dark-haired boy who is taller than the others and who unlocks the hatch into the little cabin and pulls out the two bags of sails, while the other young men, experienced but not expert sailors, pull one sail out of its bag and, with a certain nonchalance, pretending mystification and helpless inefficiency, try to figure out which sail it is and which point of the triangle should be tied to the rope that will pull it up the mast, for it is the mainsail after all, and one of the boys, finding his hands unnecessary to help with the mainsail, pulls out the jib and begins to carry it forward—only to be assaulted by the protests of his companions that he must drop the sail, that he is the guest of honor, that he should stand back and watch them work and perhaps, if he is so inclined, give them commands, sensible or not, that they will or will not follow according to their whim and which they may pretend not to hear or perhaps to misunderstand, all of this as a kindness to him in preparing him for his future which will take off on a new tack today because this one boy, shorter and huskier than the others with a wide smile and warm eyes that delight everyone who looks at him and whom you and I will pay special attention to because he is my son, a better version of myself, will this very afternoon be married, not to the kind of girl, nice as she might be, that his mother and I could have found among our friend's daughters nor a girl who takes success for granted having parents wealthier than we, but instead a beautiful girl who he says is smarter than he is, though I don't see how she could be, and who will be a wonderful wife to him as they build a life together, and, now since I have mentioned their marriage, let us leave the sailors to their morning lark for the day is clear, the wind is freshening, and the little engine that will take them out of the harbor and into the sound is humming along perfectly, and let us go ahead in time to the church where the wedding guests are assembled and where you can see me now (trying to stand up straight and relaxed as though I wore a suit all the time) in the front pew on the right with my wife of thirty-five years, looking forward, both of us, to the ceremony and to the happy life we expect our son and his bride to have and to the life we hope for as grandparents, while trying at the same time to not press this last thought on the young couple who, heaven knows, have enough to think about right now, especially as the ushers, my son's friends from college and from the sailing party this morning, show the late arrivals to their pews, as the minister steps to the front and as my son the groom, with his best man (the tall dark-haired boy) takes his place at the front of the congregation and beams down on all of us, and the organ music starts on this happiest of days that unfortunately never did happen and never will happen except repeatedly in my imagination because, when my son went to his job of only two months one morning last September, the job that promised to be the start of a wonderful career, he sat at his desk with a smile on his face and you, Mr. Bin Laden, smashed an airplane into his building.

May you rot in hell.

RIPE BERRIES
By JoRene Byers

The reason for blackberries
is so the inky bear
of our hearts
can eat fully
of summer's bounty
for the winter season.

The reason for summertime
is so the salmon
can swim upstream
to transmute
into the miracle of life.

The reason for my
being here
is simply to
swim
in this ocean
of consciousness
and smile
with purple lips,
laughing
at these
hard-to-reach
blackberries.

WHY I DIDN'T BECOME A COWBOY
By David Cook

We had driven non-stop all day, my best friend and me, from the burbs of LA where we grew up and still lived with our parents. At dusk we stopped at the first and only motel in the town. We needed our sleep because tomorrow would be our first day at Cowboy College where we would begin realizing our boyhood dreams of becoming cowboys.

First thing in the morning, we drove out of town for about an hour through some of the worst looking country I had ever seen before finally turning onto a dusty one-track lane. Over the entrance was a rustic wooden arch decorated with the words "Cowboy College" rendered in bent rebar. As we bumped down this dusty track, I was tempted to put up the top so I could close the windows. While I was contemplating this, my buddy nudged my shoulder with a concerned look on his face to inform me his cellphone was showing no service. Finally, we came to a dead end at an open area. The area was surrounded by large and small wooden buildings and fences. Behind some fences I could see horses, behind others, cows. I wrinkled my nose at the smell as I stepped out of the car. As I walked toward what I judged to be the main building, I had to keep kicking the dust out of my flipflops. I pulled open the door and followed my friend inside.

As the door closed behind us, I listened expectantly for the strum of guitars or at least a "howdy partner." Silence. My attention was drawn at last to the sound of bootsteps coming from the side.

The man wearing them appeared and asked, "You the farrier I called yesterday?"

Taken aback, it took me a minute to stammer out a "No," before clarifying, "we are here to start Cowboy College."

At that he stopped and began slowly looking us over. "Well, that mightily surprises me the way you're dressed. You have anything to wear besides those flipflops and shorts?" Before I could answer he continued, "You ever been on a horse?"

"No," I say.

"You ever seen a cow?"

"Yes, but not really up-close like," I answer.

His eyes narrowed. "Son, do you know what cowboys do?"

His questions were making me nervous, but that last one I was ready for.

"Sit around the campfire, play the guitar, sing songs, go to bars, and flirt with pretty girls," I answered with confidence.

"Yea, they might do that occasionally on their time off, which isn't often," he replied.

Back on the road to LA my buddy noted that he was finally getting a single bar on his cellphone.

"Well," he started, "Old Boots back there certainly has a way of explaining things," as he went about tuning his guitar.

"Yea," I answered dejectedly but also somewhat relieved, "now I know why I never became a cowboy and never will."

THE APOTHECARY
By Robin Emerson

A four-way friendship that lasted more than two decades began shortly after we moved into our first house. My husband and I were outside, wondering what to do about the cracked concrete driveway, when a couple walked up the street and stopped to say hello. Later we learned that Baila was in her sixties and Max, who could not have looked more vigorous, was nearing eighty. They invited us over for a drink that evening and, when we stepped into their home, we discovered they both were artists.

Baila's studio, built in a corner of their garden, was always cool and quiet. Its best feature was a wall of windows that let in the even northern light. Brushes of every size and shape, crumpled rags, scissors, scraps of paper, rolls of masking tape, and cans of solvent covered the surface of her workbench and among the clutter lay a wooden mannequin and a plaster cast of a horse's skull. Sometimes she hung her finished pieces up on the wall haphazardly as a way of tracking some developing idea. Over the years, I visited this museum of work-in-progress many times, but I'd never been invited to sit alongside her while she worked until a fall from a ladder left me with a fractured life.

Before our first meeting, I climbed into my attic to search for a tool box of art supplies from high school that had been stashed away for decades. I found it tucked under the eaves and carried it down the street to her studio so we could take an inventory. In the top tray lay some colored pencils and pastels, a few erasers, a bottle of desiccated rubber cement, and a rusty compass. In the bottom compartment we unearthed an assortment of acrylic paints. Baila picked up the cadmium red and dropped it into a trash can. "No good," she said. "Toxic." Buried among the acrylics was a tin of watercolor disks for children, along with a scraggly brush. "I want to work with watercolor," I told her. "Watercolor is difficult," she said. "You have to work fast to catch it. It's elusive. You have to have total control." I nodded. "Okay then," she said. "We'll go to Pearl Paints this week to get you what you'll need."

The following Monday, I set out my materials on the drafting table near the window. Among other things, I'd bought three sable brushes that Baila had insisted on and a box of Sakura watercolors. I didn't even know that watercolors came in tubes, but the box held twelve of them lined up in a row. By this time, I was ten months into recovery from a traumatic brain injury. I had learned to breathe without a ventilator. I had learned to swallow, eat, use the toilet, speak coherently, hold a conversation, and finally, to walk. I'd been allowed for several months to turn on the stove to boil water or heat a can of soup for lunch. Now, the terrain of healing changed. I didn't have much footing yet, but the time with Baila was for me a distillation of quiet and expansive rest.

I walked to the studio a little early on Monday mornings. I could stand on tiptoe, reach over the backyard gate, and pull the latch up to let myself in. The door to the studio was always open. Welcomed by the lingering smell of turpentine, I liked to sit in the presence of an absence and wait for Baila to arrive. When she came into the studio, she would take a long hooked pole, open the transom windows to let in air, turn on the radio, pull her rolling stool up to her canvas and settle in before she picked up a brush. She was working in oil on a large piece—maybe four feet by five—an abstract painting of two dogs playing—a mother and her pup. Planes of color, buoyant, drenched in light. It was to be her last painting, and for the hours I was there, I painted alongside her, each of us absorbed in a search for solutions.

Baila gave me direct instruction only twice—when she taught me how to clean my brushes and when she gave me a notepad of sepia-toned paper in a clothbound cover and told me to keep a journal of reflections. "Sit there," she said. "Open your notebook. Even if you don't write anything, even if you sit there for just one minute . . . same time every morning . . . what's a good time for you?" "Eight o'clock," I said. She talked about what she called the start-finish pattern. "Some interruptions are okay," she said, "but the routine is important. It's connected to regulating. It's connected to focus."

One afternoon over coffee Baila told me a story about growing up in Chicago during the Great Depression. Her father, an engineer, was unemployed so there wasn't money for painting materials. "I would never have thought to ask for them," she said. But she had crayons and pencils and was always drawing. She was ten when an older girl from the neighborhood mentioned that she was taking a life drawing class at the Art Institute of Chicago. Although art classes were out of reach, Baila tagged along. Week after week, she stood outside the classroom so that every time someone left the room she could peer inside at what the students were drawing. Then she went home and drew it. Years later, Baila ran into her childhood friend and learned that the classes had been free. "But all the months outside the classroom were a very good thing," she told me. "In that way, I learned to look. I developed a visual memory that was inherently intuitive."

I began with simple watercolors in a sketchbook. Quite of few of them were renderings of neurons and one looked vaguely like the screen of an oscilloscope. Then I tried my hand on textured cold press paper. With a pen and ruler, I drew a grid of two inch squares—twenty-five in all—and painted miniatures, some collaged from scraps clipped from the early sketches. I took a pen and ran a filament through the squares, turning the line at angles, until it reached a pinhead gap across which lay a tangled coil in the last remaining square. I called it *Pathway*.

Those twenty-five miniature paintings shared a pallor, as if faded by sunlight, bleached of liveliness, their themes more suitable for oil than for watercolor's quickness. But the intricacy of the task was self-affirming. One morning, Baila stood over my shoulder so we could look together at the finished piece. When I asked which square she liked the best, she didn't answer as expected. She pointed to one on the bottom row in which a triangle on point, orange-smudged and oblique, its edges barely discernible, tipped away from a red post, its balance precarious. She said that it was brave.

Baila gave me a prescription: "Don't be shy of failure." When I started anew, I painted without plan or expectation. What could come from a wild tincture of paint and water? After the pools of color dried, I cut out a section where fuchsia, bottle-green, deep-blue and amber folded into furrows. There are memories in the painting. I named the colors after them:

The bell-like petals of a hanging plant, a scrub jay's call nearby
An algae skin beneath the ripples of a shallow, spring-fed stream
Dante's sky before the sunrise on the mountain
A necklace brought back home from Warsaw by my father

I took a needle and some black thread and stitched a curve into the paper. Then, with a length of red thread, I tied a fisherman's fly at one end and glued it to the paper in a wandering line. Baila said, "I like the knot." I called the portrait *Suture*.

One afternoon, less than a year after we'd begun our Monday meetings, I answered a knock on the door. A woman I didn't recognize was standing on my front porch. There was a hint of amusement in her eyes and she stood there expectantly as if waiting for me to say something. She was an older woman, petite, with dark, glossy hair cut in a chin-length bob. Who was this stranger who looked oddly familiar? I'm sure I looked perplexed. "I'm Barbara," the woman said. "I'm here from Chicago visiting Baila, and I wanted to meet you." I took a closer look and laughed. Before the chemo, Baila wore her silver hair clipped close to her scalp. Now her bald head was covered with a wig. She had told me of the diagnosis over the phone a few weeks before. Brain cancer. "I didn't want to tell you," she said. I remember it as a quiet conversation when the noise of the world fell away. By the following spring, at the age of eighty-five, she was dead.

In her personal life, Baila projected warmth and a gentle humor. Her chief quality was an unspoken inquisitiveness, an attunement to the people around her and to the world in its confused and aching woundedness. Possessed of a natural vibrancy, she seemed utterly without self-consciousness. Whatever the heartbreak in her life, she never spoke of it with me. But in another sense, she did. She drew, painted, sculpted without compromise, naming equally the good and bad. Within her work resided both the sacred and peculiar, the grain of sand within the oyster shell—what C.G. Jung referred to as the tension of the opposites.

Baila placed her last sculpture in the garden near a trellis overgrown with honeysuckle. *The Horse Dancer.* Cast in bronze. Rough surface, blue patina. The attenuated bodies of the horse and dancer made me think of Giacometti—but while his work is of earth, hers is air. The dancer, caught mid-motion, arms lifted overhead, turns toward the horse, and the horse has turned toward her. No horse, but this one, could twist its neck so far around in such a graceful curve. I see reconciliation in the dance, the end of yearning, a pause caught in its fullest gesture.

I remember a day in the studio when Baila rolled back on her stool and sat there looking at her canvas of the mother and her pup. I put down my brush to watch. She and the canvas were talking. "It looks finished to me," I said after awhile. "Why would you want to change anything? What would you change?" She looked thoughtful for a moment. "Sometimes you paint out an area even though you don't know what will come through next," she said. "Sometimes *what's to be seen* and *what looks* fall in love. Then the *not yet seen* appears. When I'm working on a piece, there's a battle going on. It's literally a battleground. And you can shed blood and tears. There's a merging that takes place. I'm in the work and the work is in me."

Eleven years after her death, I can look up from my desk and see the simple pen-and-ink drawing she gave me before she died. It's a study of a stalk of Mexican bush sage against an empty field of white. The space between the branching spikes is filled with tiny hatch marks and embedded there, almost invisible, is the faint trace of her signature.

SAND DOLLAR PAIRING
By Carol Barrett

    i

Mating is a wet story. Females release
eggs in the ocean company of males.
Conjoined eggs float out in a salty
calling, drop to seafloor, build silvered
shells, threading plankton through cilia
to mouths smaller than a cervix. They feed
six to ten years, adding rings, like trees.

When they roll ashore upside down,
they dig an edge in, wait for a wave's
mercy. They understand waiting.
Tradition has it, the star on the front,
born of the night sky of Bethlehem,
feathered tracing on the back, poinsettia.

    ii

All his life he's hunted the beach.
Young summers he looked for a whole one,
traipsing miles of sand, dreams broken
over and over with the rumbling tides,
gulls piercing the wind, dunes crumbling.
Working in shadow boxes, he's become
a sand dollar artist, two thousand now
catalogued in his garage, eleven species.

Each new find, he imagines the scene,
watery backdrops banked by pebbles.

Someone needs what he'll place
in this empty box given up
to a thrift store. A mooring, a harbor
of hope, bits of polished blue glass
reflecting angelic light, the center
star emanating rays of wonder, a slow
coming in the sand for a barren womb.

A DATE WITH THE HIRWAS
By Seetharam Dravida

The two-hour picturesque drive to Ruhengeri from Kigali early in the morning was breathtaking. The wind blew in from the north, across the open fields and distant rows of trees. Despite the sun edging over the mountains to the east, casting back shadows and coloring in the spaces, the wind still carried the last traces of a cold night. It was 7 am. Thoughts about the day started streaming into my mind as I arrived at the visitor center.

My eyes widened at the sight of the volcanoes as I got out of my car.

The Volcanoes National Park is home to five of the eight volcanoes in the Virunga mountains—Karisimgi (14,787ft), Muhabana (13,540 ft), Bioske (12,175 ft), Sabyinyo (12,037ft), and Gahinga (11,398 ft). Mount Bisoke is the only active volcano, the rest being dormant. The National park is home to golden monkeys and some very rare gorillas—especially in Mountain Sabyinyo, an extinct volcano in the Virunga range, whose peak resembles the worn-out teeth of an older man.

The other visitors also arrived by 7:30 am. After the registration process, I joined a group of seniors with a similar age profile. I carried a small backpack with a few snacks and a water bottle. Two young forest guides took an hour to provide us with a detailed briefing, with a few dos and don'ts, sign language guidance, and even a few sounds we could make to communicate with the gorillas.

The briefing concluded with a few details about the Hirwa gorilla family.

Hirwa means "the lucky ones" in native Kinyarwanda. This family came into existence when Munyinga, the dominant silverback, got into trouble with the Susa family for constantly mating with their females, and decided to leave his family with two females. He moved to Mountain Sabyinyo collecting other females with him along the way. The Hirwa gorilla family is regarded as lucky, as one of the births resulted in a set of twins.

In addition to two guides, we were accompanied by four porters and four forest rangers. The porters carried our backpacks and helped us navigate the rough patches on the trek. Each of us was given a solid stick as support for the climb.

After the briefing by the guides, we boarded our jeeps and traveled for two kilometers over stones and gravel. Real stones! We got down after the two-kilometer Jeep journey and began our trek on a narrow pathway nestled between Irish potato fields. I could get a bird's eye view of the diverse local flora and fauna while walking the narrow trail. After thirty minutes, our guides provided us with additional briefing while the forest rangers marched ahead to locate the family.

The trail was rough, with ups and downs through a tropical jungle. The porters had to physically lift and put me onto the track at some places. After an hour of climbing, it seemed impossible to go further. I felt powerless, my body became unresponsive. In some areas, I remember crawling forward on my knees, inch by inch. Both the guides gave me enough time, waited for me, and motivated me to continue with the trek. I learned that many visitors would give up at this point and return to the base.

The rangers cleared the bushes and twigs and made some paths for us to move further. After another hour, a ranger brought good news. He had sighted a Hirwa family member nearby. While the information made me happy, I was exhausted and did not want to proceed further. After fifteen minutes, another ranger approached us urgently and asked us to offload all our stuff, including the walking sticks. We could carry our phones and cameras only. He strictly requested us not to talk or make noises, as he had had a sighting. I found out that I was to lead the team from the front and make contact with the first gorilla family member. Of course, the guide would be walking right next to me.

I fell suddenly still when I saw the first gorilla. I raised my eyebrows and made greeting gestures. The baby gorilla stared. She stood still, and I was terrified that she would jump on me. After surveying me briefly, she played, fed, and bounced around from one branch to the other on a nearby tree. Another baby gorilla joined her, and the guide told me that they were twin siblings and three years old. Other members of my team came forward at this time. As we took photos with our phones, the mother entered the arena. She was a massive animal with considerable weight. My guide asked me to step aside so that the mother could have direct access to her babies. It was a treat to watch them in the forest.

Soon, another family member arrived from somewhere behind us. This gorilla was a giant, and we thought she would surely jump on us. Nothing like that happened. All the family members started walking down a path, and we started following them from a distance. Suddenly four more descended from nowhere and joined the group. These were reasonably big. Then Munyinga—the father, and the only silver streaked gorilla in the group, arrived on the scene. The silver streak on his back glistened in the sun. The guide told me that he was thirty-seven years old and the mother was thirty-one.

As soon as the head of the family arrived, the other members became busy, playing, feeding, and talking to each other, similar to a human family. Someone was hitting their chest, another was helping the little ones climb, and a few of the others were making strange noises. I am sure they were discussing important family issues among themselves. It was such a pleasure to see them interact with each other.

We spent about an hour with the Hirwa family. A rare sense of joy, and anxiety filled my mind. Then the time came to say goodbye. All of us in the group took last-minute photographs and sounded a formal parting note. The Hirwa family continues to live happily in the mountains, and I am sure the members have their own set of life challenges. They live, play, communicate with each other, and express love with simplicity. They have no mobile phones and no internet to worry about, no bosses to listen to and no calendars to follow!

I learnt the simple joys of life from these lovely creatures.

DIAMOND SUE, OREGON
A Novel Excerpt by Scott Stewart

Highway 140 mile markers count the distance down across an expanse so full of nothing your heart aches for all of it. Crazy! For hours.

Then curving down off the ridge, a gas station sign: twenty miles—the annunciation of life out here—nectar for a town, restless ions, without it only a matter of time.

Diamond Sue, Oregon, pop 85. Gas station, bar, store, gem shop, bar, motel, laundromat.

But it's the side streets you notice, a block long, old low houses and single-wides, wind-gnarled fence posts bowed flat to the ground, then sand, rock, sagebrush, and a magnified distance scrambling near and far.

Streets end with tire tracks that can't decide, plowing thirty feet out then turning back around in the weeds.

The tracks blend back into the dusty street to one bar or the other. This one feels good, cushioned armrests and ashtrays, nobody cares if you smoke in here, take pride in it actually, fuck Salem, so you buy a pack of Camel unfiltered and an Old Crow neat and hang with the town.

They smell the Portland on you, but please and thanks for the mustard and ketchup goes a ways, along with the fact that you're actually smoking that Camel.

It's amazing what a little obtrusive fitting-in will do, and they say the motel's ok if you don't mind the truck noise and the other bar has a better breakfast, and it's a fine time drinking and smoking with a world outside the buildings you're hubristically tempted to think they don't see.

Sun goes down and the wind is brutally cold on the side street where you parked, "Paiute Avenue," peeling off a building slat. Nothing here traps heat and the air powering through was a thousand miles north yesterday, purified by its journey and it blows right through you almost as if you weren't there because you're so close, only a few yards, from the beginnings of no boundary at all. Your slightest change in feeling ricochets unhindered through the domed space, a random pinball route rebounding through whirlygigged sounds and lightbulb arpeggios lying just beneath the stars' stillness.

There's endless room for that here, a smallest intent made gigantic by all the indifferent night sky it has to fill, and a brush of your thumb on the flipper button sends it off all over again until the beginning hue of unobstructed astronomical dawn locks the arcade for the night. Day arrives, shuts the engine off, and sleeps in the backseat for a couple hours before punching in.

***

The next night, somnambulant: digital 2:15 a.m. rising from roseate blur into red focus, adrift for that split-second when you don't know where you are until a gray brush, swiping the black surfaces, stops to detail the ridge line of your clothes hanging over the chair. I want to see out there.

New moon, or close. The smallest sliver erasing itself right now. You hate to desecrate the street with your flashlight, but, dude, it's dark out here. Get where you're going and turn it off. I know where I'm going before I know, and my boots crunch the volcanic gravel on the traverses up to the gem shop on top of the knoll. I find an empty five-gallon plastic bucket, turn it over, sit, and slide the thumb-switch off. The dark weight of night-dome and no-moon thumps down on my flashlight-constricted irises and the whole Cimmerian world relaxes as they do. West, low wattage security lights around the gas pumps twinkle like small silver Christmas bulbs. In one house across from the other bar maybe a microwave clock is the curtain's blue illumine. The quiet here is immense, pining for the furthest extent of silence, as others have for 15,000 years.

Once all the surrounding blackness was water, a deep inland sea, waxing and waning in size like a moon cycle over countless Kalpas. The high places were its shorelines, which grew in recent millennia as the waters receded. Now it was nearly all shore, with a few shallow, dicey lakes and marshes scattered in its deepest places like those nearby. Enough to feed small aboriginal bands that ranged over the area up to 200 years ago, summoned by sparse manna appearing in different places through the seasons.

I love the dark and its apophatic new moon. The blue sky tomorrow will hold me in its necessary and desirable companionships, but this, right now—night-emptied—*is* me. There is no deeper version.

What is this place, square corners and built lines barely visible now, set in nothing. Maybe a sangha, an arrow of irregularly attached blocks pointing deeper into the wasteland, after all.

FRIDAY NIGHTS

By Cameron Prow

I labor past five
finishing tasks I used to put off until Monday,
driving back roads that curve around the morning freeways to work.
I stop for pedestrians not in crosswalks,
linger nose-deep in bouquets waiting hopefully against checkout walls.

Tonight, I let one six-pack crowd ahead of
my laundry soap, cat litter, and
single-serving soups.
The bagger walks me to my car,
his biceps flexing as he lays my prosaic parcels on the
back seat where I first saw "Gone With the Wind."

I drive home in twilight
sliding into silken shadows,
haunted by forever moments of butterfly men.

TECHNICAL FOUL
By Randy Workman

I rather pride myself on my technological prowess. My house is almost fully automated. So good am I that I have renamed my eavesdropping big-tech company products. I use the name Ruby instead of their given names. *Goodnight Ruby* and all the lights throughout the house turn off, doors lock, and shades automatically close. At the appropriate time I command the floors be cleaned, and the robotic vacuum whirls into action, moving deftly around furniture.

Whether I'm away from home or molded into the sofa with a book, I can use my phone to execute the same magic powers to requisition assistance or service.

Ruby play Frank Zappa's "Montana." The kids used to get a kick out of this song. When people asked my son what he wanted to be when he grew up, he'd tell them he was going to be a dental floss farmer. Then they would look to me and I'd have to explain that was Zappa's song.

But, hey that was Zappa. Years ago, when I outgrew The Monkees and a friend set the needle down on "WPLJ" from The Mothers Invention's *Burnt Weeny Sandwich* album, I became a Frank Zappa fan.

I suspect I shared my story of Zappa being my first concert and Tom Waits as the opening act a few times too many. When my son came across a framed poster from the 1960s of Frank Zappa sitting on the toilet, he presented it to me as a Father's Day gift years ago. Since that day it has always had a place on our walls somewhere in the house.

For the first time in almost two years the kids were coming by. I thought I would surprise the gang with my specialty butterscotch cookies. Around the kitchen counter I unfurled all the ingredients, the mixing bowl, and a spatula.

I dismissed my rumbling stomach. I was on a mission. I envisioned a storybook family reunion accompanied by a sweet cooking aroma wafting through the house. I rolled out my cookies and placed them into perfect petite dough balls.

Again, with the stomach. The ol' breadbasket continued to flip and flop for no particular reason I could think of, so I continued to dismiss it. The oven was properly preheated and I anticipated the aroma of fresh baked cookies filling the house.

The warnings were over. Immediate action was required. My stomach didn't take kindly to being ignored. I quickly stuffed the cookie tray into the oven letting the oven door bang shut.

Oh man.

I rapidly penguin walked with one hand holding my buttocks together. I reached the bathroom not a second too soon. I tossed my cell phone to the floor.

Disaster averted, so I thought.

Once my phone crashed landed, it sent out emergency alerts to my wife, son, daughter-in-law, emergency services, and the next-door neighbor. Three urgent texts messages were sent:

I NEED HELP!!

PLEASE HELP ME!!

The third text was a picture of me sitting on the toilet with my pants around my ankles, accompanied by a map locator, all courtesy of my sorcerer's assistant.

The phone rang, the doorbell chimed, my son ran into the house and pounded on the bathroom door.

"Are you okay?" he yelled.

"I am fine," I replied from behind the door.

The smoldering smell of burnt butterscotch activated the trilling smoke alarm with a volume akin to the Grateful Dead's "Wall of Sound" speakers. I washed my hands, left the bathroom, and headed toward the kitchen just as the fire department rolled up. Curious neighbors lined the sidewalk. I turned off the oven and went out to tell the fire captain what happened. Apparently she already knew, stifling a laugh as the text picture arrived of me in the bathroom. As word spread the neighbors dispersed, their laughter audible from down the street.

Today sharing wall space with the Frank Zappa poster is a framed photo of me in the same imprudent position.

"A" IS FOR ALZHEIMER'S
By Niki Rainwater

"Fran is getting into Alzheimer's," my father tells me over the phone, as if she has suddenly taken up golf. Divided by 500 miles, politics, and Covid, we talk daily.

At eighty-eight, my father has outlived one sibling, two wives, and most of his friends. His once immaculate house is now a carnival of junk mail, stacked randomly on every flat surface, including the stove top. I can hear papers shuffle through the receiver.

"Dad?"

"Pardon?" He inadvertently hits the FaceTime button, and his left ear becomes a topographic map, which fills the screen. "I'm looking for my pen. I need to make a note about Fran."

"Dad?"

"You don't know this, but salmon is good for helping with memory loss." *What I truly don't know is why my father has recently started to bridge each fresh topic of conversation with this lead in. I know I shouldn't, but I bite the hook every time.*

"I'm sixty-two years old, Dad, of course I know the health benefits of eating salmon. And you hit the FaceTime button!" *Dad, do you know that!?* I've raced through a wormhole, and I am my teenage self again in light seconds. *And what about Fran?*

"Pardon?"

As he fiddles with his phone I glimpse his paper strewn sofa, like the contents of a 1950s time capsule. Since unearthing his high school yearbooks from mildewed cardboard, they snuggle next to him on the sofa. Close, like a prom date.

"What?" my father says. He can't hear me. His iPhone might as well be alien technology. This once brilliant civil engineer has surrendered to the cobwebs of time.

"Dad, look at the phone!" *Breathe. Reset.* His upper lip and right nostril are now in view, like an abstract painting. We're making progress now.

"I didn't know you liked salmon . . . ?"

"Well, sure I do!" I can hear his voice tighten as he says this. I realize that his fear of dementia has overruled the demands of his taste buds. My father was fifty before a single bite of seafood passed his lips, and now he's an authority on the health benefits of fish.

He regales the day's events (domestic and international) according to Fox News, then moves on to his favorite topic: how Jerry Brown ruined California. He has retold this story for over three decades. In my father's mind, it's on par with the sinking of Titanic.

"That's all. Love you. Good night, Honey."

"Good night, Dad. Love you."

I lean back on the sofa. Outside it's snowing. I hear my mother's voice, *"breathe."* Somewhere deep in our collective fiber is woven a fierce kind of love. I close my eyes and imagine the present scene on Dad's sofa. Poor Fran. "A" for Alzheimer's, a freshly noted abbreviation next to her yearbook photo. Turn the page and there she is, her soft eyes gaze out from the yellowed page. My beautiful mother in her cap and gown. "D" for deceased, noted in faded ink.

ENCOUNTER
By Krayna Castelbaum

I stand alone at a bus stop.
    Blistering heat. No breeze stirs.
        No sprinklers swish.
    No mowers hum. Just sun
scorched thick silence.
    My eyes bore into the tired ground
        below my feet.
    A sudden chill
forces my head to lift. Across the street
    beside a white house with white curtains
        in the tall weeds of a forsaken yard
    stands my father
whose ashes rest in a jet-black container
    on a shelf in my mother's hall closet.
        He stares at me, blank-faced.
    Something in me tilts.
I stare back, stunned
    that I'm not glad
        to see him again.
    Eyes locked on mine
he strides toward me slowly
    then picks up speed,
        drab gray coattails flying
    behind him, arms flapping up and down,
quiet as a dark-winged owl
    taking flight.

    I'm stiff as a tree limb encased
  in ice. A thought explodes in my mind—
he's going to crash into me!
    But my father, or whatever this is,
        blows through me, leaving behind
    nothing but a disturbance
of air on my bone-cold skin.

HARRY CAN'T
By Jake Sheaffer

Occasional snowflakes fell through the barren branches of a withered maple tree onto Harry's wrinkled cheeks and frost-nipped reddened nose. The flakes melted in moments of landing on his skin. Only leaving the tickle of water at the tip of his nose and along the edge of his chin.

When the moisture became too much for him to ignore, he ran a now dampened handkerchief past where the water playfully agitated his face. The same way that his mother did when Harry and Beth played with their dad in the snow as children. Harry took in a deep breath and then let out a long exhale at the memory.

Across a soft uphill lawn, Harry gazed at his kid sister's festive home. The front door was wreathed in fresh garland, and the gutters were lined with strands of gentle white lights. Beth and her husband, Levi, had a wonderful knack for timeless holiday designs. Harry felt a smile come over him as he stared at the decorations, but the physical manifestation didn't follow.

Hidden under the shadow of the maple tree from the holiday lighting, Harry tried time and again to find the courage to walk to the front door and just knock.

In the past hour, on a rapidly cooling metal bench, Harry pictured himself raising the elegantly curved knocker on its hinge and bringing it down twice against the brass plate in quick succession to announce his arrival to Beth and the rest of the family. The image would continue with someone greeting him at the door; he hoped it would be his sister, Beth, or her oldest boy, Asher. He must be ten now, Harry thought. This daydream and the subsequent warm holiday greetings they would share with one another replayed in his head more times than there were snowflakes on the ground. In a few of these holiday dreams, he even saw his father coming down the high banister staircase, wearing a jubilant smile and a cozy holiday sweater. Harry and he would give one another a smiling nod in this fantasy, and like that, over a half-decade of animosity would melt away.

That scene dissolved, giving way to reality.

Heavier and wetter snow started to fall. Most of it landed on the lawn and above Harry, in the tree's boughs, but some found its way through the naked branches to lay on his shoulders and thighs and along the edges of the garden bench he sat on. Harry gave his body a half-hearted shake to remove the snow.

"What's another day anyway?" Harry asked himself with a languished breath, no longer looking at the front door. "I can just come by tomorrow when it's just Beth and her family."

Harry let his neck go limp and tilt backward, towards the night sky.

Faint lines of clouds swayed and twirled against the dark sky. Their movement reminded Harry of how his mother's dress would swish around when she and his father danced in the living room to the old vinyl records of their youth. Those memories were from when Harry idolized his father.

As time passed by and the night got colder, Harry tracked single snowflakes from as far up as possible and followed them until they fell past his periphery. After he counted his one-hundredth, his torso and legs let out a vigorous shiver without warning.

"Brrrrr!" Harry responded instinctively, but he continued to let the snow pile on and around him.

"Hi, Uncle Harry," an excited child's voice said.

Harry's neck and head tilted down till his eyes were level with a young boy.

Most of the kid's face remained backlit from Beth's house, but enough light bent around him that Harry recognized his oldest nephew, Asher.

He wore a thick woolen toboggan that looked comical, making Harry smile. The hat managed to cover most of Asher's wavy blond hair, but some of the strands poked out like golden springs. A trait he shared with Beth and his grandfather.

"Asher?" Harry asked rhetorically. His oldest nephew nodded his head with enthusiasm. "But you're not supposed to be this tall, not until you're at least ten," he said with a wink and smile. Asher laughed.

Harry leaned forward when his nephew laughed. A lot of the cold snow sloughed off his shoulders while he brushed off what had accumulated on his thighs when he did.

"I'm eleven, Uncle Harry," Asher explained at the end of his laugh.

"Eleven? But that can't be so. You're far too tall to be just eleven."

Nephew and uncle smiled at Harry's jestful question.

A form of Harry's imagined scenes from before became a reality, but so did the frigidness of his dampened clothes that he had been ignoring. He hid his shivers from Asher as best as possible.

Harry saw the front door swing open and a woman's figure step out from over Asher's shoulder. His nephew turned his neck to see her hand beckon to the two of them. Harry massaged his hands together for warmth when his nephew looked away. Asher waved back to her and nodded his head, then looked back to his uncle.

"Oh, that's right," Asher said with realization in his voice and on his face. "Mom told me to tell you to come inside and join us like you said you would." He brushed an especially pronounced hair curl away from his left eye and tucked it under his hat.

Harry leaned back into the shadow and gave Asher's message from his mom a shy smile.

"She did, did she?" Harry asked another rhetorical question, but Asher answered regardless with an enthusiastic, "Yep."

"What did your Grandpa say?"

Asher responded with a shrug but added, "Nothing, really. He's mostly been in the kitchen talking to my dad about boring stuff."

Harry's head and whole body nodded along with Asher's response.

"Sounds good, thanks, kiddo. Tell your mom I'll be in in a few. Sound good?"

"Okay, see you inside, Uncle Harry. Grandpa got Noah and Everett some fun presents you might find fun also. Mom also said that supper's almost ready, or well, it's probably ready now," Asher explained. His voice and attitude never changed from his initial hello.

Small footprints followed the boy through the yard and up to the front door. Asher turned back to see if his uncle had followed him.

Harry faked a smile for himself and waved his gloved hand forward to get Asher to go inside.

Once his nephew closed the door behind himself, Harry went back to the sky above as he attempted to recapture those imagined moments from before. Sometimes he grabbed ahold of one of those idyllic family scenes around the dinner table, but the nettled sting of his frigid hands inside of his all but frozen gloves caused him too much pain. The faces of his nephews, brother-in-law, Beth, and even his father became a blur as his body went into an uncontrollable quiver.

"Asher said you were right behind him twenty minutes ago," a stern and disquiet voice said.

Harry didn't rush to tilt his shaky head down, but when he did, he saw Beth standing there with her hands tucked deep into coat pockets while her wavy blond hair was exposed to the night. Beth had fixed one side of her hair into a lovely single braid that imitated a forest fern and pinned back the other with a holiday-styled brooch that Harry recognized immediately. Their mother wore the pin every holiday season. Pleased to see the heirloom, Harry gave a genuine smile; his teeth chattered along with the shake of his body.

"Hey Beth, yeah, sorry . . . I was just thinking some, and well, the night felt, um, nice," Harry stammered out.

Beth cocked her head, "Come on inside, Harry, dinner is hot, and the boys are excited to see you. Levi always enjoys your company, and I want to spend the holiday with my big brother." Her voice cracked at the end.

Under his coat, Harry felt for the three soft bumps where he kept the gifts for his nephews tucked away. He felt a bit silly bringing gifts to kids he hadn't seen in a few years, but he knew presents were in the job description of being an uncle.

"Come on, I'm getting cold out here, and I can tell you're freezing," Beth said, nodding towards the house.

"What did Dad say?" Harry asked.

Beth's shoulders sighed heavier than her voice did at the question.

"Nothing. He's playing with his grandchildren and drinking eggnog."

In the limited light, Harry saw the mix of frustration and love on his sister's face. He controlled the shake of his head and nodded.

Harry reached out for Beth and placed his other hand on his numbed leg to push off. Beth grabbed his outstretched hand, and with her help, Harry stood up.

The two of them walked shoulder to shoulder. Beth kept at Harry's slowed pace as they went up the yard.

Harry's body reacted to the abrupt movement with a short but distressing shudder. He slipped on a slick patch of snow at the sudden shock to his body. Beth kept him from falling with a hand under his forearm and her other arm wrapped around his shoulders.

"Thanks," Harry said and regained his balance with the aid of his sister.

"Anytime," Beth said as they approached the wide bay window that looked into the living room.

Inside, Harry saw his three nephews playing with their dad and their unwrapped gifts. He patted the spot where he kept his gifts to them. Harry felt glad that he had come tonight, but then he saw his father walk into the living room, full cocktail glass in hand. His blonde wavy hair had turned gray since the last time Harry had seen his father, but the hardness of his face and eyes remained ageless to Harry.

Harry stopped walking. He looked at Beth, and she gave a gentle tug on his arm.

"Harry, it'll be okay, he promised me," Beth pleaded with Harry.

"I'm sorry, Beth, I just can't," Harry said in a rush as he shoved the gifts into Beth's empty hands. He turned away from the house.

The crunch of the snow underneath his boots muffled his sister's beseeched voice.

WHAT'S IN IT FOR THE RIVER
By Ellen Waterston

In the shadow of no rain, in this brittle-boned
desert we call home, we strut and fret on a stage
of basaltic sponge.

For volcanic eons, paleo to present, the desert
has banked water to loan to steelhead, frog, salmon—
and the likes of you and I who've filled our thirsty cups
to green home and working lands at the expense of wild.

The liquid currency of river, stream and lake rises
unbidden from deep under to straight arrow, meander,
and ox bow, meting out liquid nutrition on course
to the ocean.

We two-leggeds describe this cycle as though we invented it;
as though the river didn't know it until we got here to tell it,
showed up to interrupt it; as though we're separate
from the ways of water, but we're not.

Not from vapor, cloud, or dew. Not from watery passages far or here . . .
such beauties as Metolius, Whychus, Deschutes. If we see ourselves
as unconnected, might just as well tie a tourniquet around our bobbing,
naked hearts, stop the throbbing current, eclipse the moon tides
that rise inside us.

For we are of the rivers and oceans born. We've come full, slow,
crooked circle to a Native wisdom here long before. At last
we're moved to ask: What's in it for the river? What return
on its generous advance, its fund of trust, its freedom from interest?

What is in it for the river? We know the aquifer is overdrawn, spent.
Unless we raise the balance in this artesian basin, raise the rate
of saturation, pay back the liquid with our gold, our attention,
the answer to the river is: Not much.

TRANSPLACE

By Denice Hughes Lewis

Jarill snuck out of bed and stared at herself in the reflective walls of her sleeping quarters. Light purple skin, everything else black—form-fitting uniform, eyes, long hair. Nothing special. So why did Tarron choose her?

She crept past her sib's bed.

"Shall I tell Maz you're sneaking out?"

Startled, Jarill glared at Aronna. "Want your secrets kept?"

Aronna smirked. "Fair enough. Don't do anything stupid."

"Great advice from the master."

Ducking the thrown pillow, Jarill slid open the suite door manually to avoid the hum of the auto-meck system. She squeezed through and tiptoed across the dimly-lit central living chamber. One more door. Slender fingers pried it open.

Jarill slipped into the empty maze of the spacecraft's transit tubes. Her hand instinctively flicked toward the IPT unit in her pocket. She dared not use it for instantaneous transport or the sensors would pick her up. Though it was required that everyone be in zizz-sleep except those running the ship at night, Jarill worried about being discovered on the way to her destination deep inside the vessel. After all, she wasn't asleep.

Moisture seeped down her neck. She could not possibly be hot. No Ice Lord ever suffered heat, accustomed to the frigid lands of their home planet, Zirrekk. Stupid nerves.

Jarill frowned when purified air assaulted her senses. How she missed the fresh, sweet breezes, moist soil, scents of a world she would never see again. She swallowed the bitter taste in her mouth at the memory of leaving home. Maz and Daz leaped at the opportunity to explore space. Aronna agreed only because her intended partner-match rejected her. Fourteen seasons of Jarill's life carried little weight when she protested. They ripped her away from her fonds, her elders, her beloved granmaz, and forced her to live on a spaceship with strangers. She might have accepted the decision if her planet were dying, diseased, or overpopulated. Never voluntary exploration of the universe. Two seasons of her life had already been stolen.

Jarill scowled out the massive windows of the transit tube into unlimited space. Star clusters and several bright planets did nothing to appease her. Nor the beauty of their spacecraft. A hundred giant, metal and crystal pillars jutted in every direction—luminous and hurtling at a tremendous speed to an unknown destination. She moved forward, hiding in the shadows of space that crept across the metal floor of her flying prison.

She didn't know if she trembled from fear or excitement as she raced down corridors that led to her meeting with Tarron: the only one who paid attention to her, the only one who made her life worth living. Her granmaz's last words drifted into her mind. "Remember you are worthy of your own life. Do not rely on anyone for your happiness."

Jarill whispered, "I have to, Granmaz, or lose my mind."

She finally reached an almost-hidden door and removed her three-star crystal earring to light the way. Smaller, inky tunnels led her deeper into the belly of the ship. She reached the entrance to the Secondary Interface Station—a perfect place to meet away from prying eyes. Smoothing her hair, she took a deep breath and stepped inside.

Two chairs faced the wall-to-ceiling electronic panels. Tables clustered before color-coded lights, indicator switches, and levers perched between dozens of monitors that displayed the cosmos from every angle of the ship. A billion stars shimmered in vast space. Awe took her breath away.

Tarron pulled her into his arms. "Am I not important enough for you to be on time?"

She stared into the violet eyes of the handsome son of Ambassador Ryokk. His cropped silver hair, high cheekbones, and muscled body tempted every unattached fem on the ship.

She smiled. "Worried I wouldn't come?"

He chuckled and pulled her closer, gently kissing one cheek, the other, her nose. Tingles streaked through her body in waves of longing when he reached her mouth. His lips tasted of sweet and spicy berreez.

Her lips melted, soft and pliable under his, until she forced herself to pull away. He must not know how much she needed him.

He grinned. "No one can hide their feelings from me. Especially you."

"Get out of my mind."

He laughed. "You know I don't read minds."

With burning cheeks, she yanked away when he tried to kiss her again. "How is trespassing into my feelings any different?"

Tarron raised one silver eyebrow. "It is as natural to me as breathing."

"You are the only person on the ship with such a gift. What if I invaded your emotions?"

He ran a finger down her cheek. "You have."

She stalked away from him. "It's not the same. What you do is dishonorable."

He stiffened. "No one speaks to me like that."

"Someone has to."

He threw himself in a chair, violet eyes dark with anger. "No one would dare."

She grabbed his hand. "Didn't anyone teach you control?"

"Several guardians tried. My faz encourages my gift. He considers it extremely useful in his position."

Jarill shook her head. "That doesn't make it right."

"You have no idea how difficult it is to be the Ambassador's son. It's not my choice to inherit my father's position." He pulled her onto his lap and whispered into her hair. "How I envy your freedom."

"It might be different when our Commander decides to colonize a planet instead of exploring the whole frackling cosmos," she said.

"You do not know my faz."

She knew enough to be glad the Ambassador wasn't related to her. Thoughts of his stern, sharp-face were interrupted by a small beep.

Jarill leapt out of his arms. "What's that noise?" She whirled to locate the sound. "There." One yellow light pulsed irritably on a lower panel.

"Nothing to concern us. Central Control is quite capable of handling the minute details of running our ship."

"Why haven't they?" Nerves twitching in her fingers, she pressed buttons and scrolled over the timetables. Unease slivered down her neck. "This started seven suns ago."

"Are you sure?"

"I grew up watching my maz transcribe interstellar phenomenon. I think this section relates to deep space."

Terron chuckled. "Beauty and intelligence, an enticing combination." His hand caressed her cheek before he leaned in to kiss her.

She pulled away. "The ship might be in danger. I have to talk to Maz." She checked the monitors, found the panel for the ship's communication system, and entered Maz's private code.

"Do you have any idea what my faz will do if he finds us together?"

"Then go."

His face hardened and he tugged her toward the door. "You're coming with me."

She slugged his arm.

"Hey."

"I'm sorry. The ship's safety is more important."

Maz's voice boomed from the communicator panel. "Jarill. You are not in your room. Where are you?"

She would not lie and took a shaky breath. "The Secondary Interface Station."

"Your daz will be furious."

Jarill forgot it was his turn to pilot the ship. "Maz, listen to me. There's a flashing yellow light on the section that warns of interstellar anomalies."

"I will call you back after I check with your daz."

Nervous as the wild jaguarats locked in the holds, Jarill flinched when the beeps changed to red and grew more insistent.

Tarron turned her to face him. "I'm sorry for not taking you seriously."

"I'm used to it."

Time dragged, unlike the racing of her heart.

"Jarill?"

She hardly recognized Maz's tear-filled voice. "Here. What's happening?"

"The corresponding section malfunctioned in Central Control Navigation. The crew missed the warning. After quick calculations, your daz discovered the problem. A fast-moving black hole crashed into an asteroid, changing its course. It's headed toward us at 900 million miles an hour."

"Are we in danger?" Tarron asked.

"Who's that with you?"

Jarill winced. "Ambassador Ryokk's son."

Maz sighed softly. "The pilots conferred and decided to use SurgeThrust to implement a gravity-assist trajectory around the nearest sun. They hope to lessen the impact."

Jarill quivered. "The asteroid is going to hit us?"

Tarron's light purple face paled to silver. "What is the projected survival rate?"

"Sixty percent if the ship survives the collision and lands safely."

Uneasy heartbeats jabbed into the walls of Jarill's chest. "Four hundred of us will die?"

"We have warned everyone to do what they can to ensure their safety."

"How long, Maz?"

"Not long enough."

"I will be up as fast as I can."

"No. Both of you stay there."

"But Maz, I want to be with—"

"As your superior officer, I command you to remain where you are. It is the safest place on the ship."

Panels, screens, and a mass of colors whirled before Jarill's eyes. Her knees buckled.

Tarron caught her before she fell. "Steady."

Maz's muted voice floated into her unaccepting mind. "Secure yourselves. And Jarill?"

Jarill's voice caught in her throat. "Y-yes?"

"You have the strongest will in our family. I believe in you. Never forget that. You can do anything. Whatever happens, remember, I love you."

Jarill doubled over, spikes twisting her stomach. How could this be happening? Fear smothered her senses. "Maz, I love you so much. Tell Daz and Aronna."

She staggered toward the monitors to observe the deadly asteroid hurtling toward the ship. The gigantic, irregular mass of ugly gray rock grew larger. So did her feelings of helpless insignificance. She buried her face against Tarron's shoulder. "I haven't started living."

He held her tight. "There is always hope. We will survive."

She took comfort in his words, wanting to believe the lie.

The ship hit SurgeThrust, slamming them to the floor. They scrambled to lock themselves into the chair harnesses.

Empty blackness filled Jarill's mind like the lifeless craters that gouged the enormous asteroid.

"Where do you think it will hit us?" Tarron asked.

"Depends on our velocity and its relationship to the asteroid's speed."

"You are very young to know this."

She bit her lip. "Too young."

The spacecraft shifted sideways under them.

Jarill's eyes raced across the panels. "We've reached gravity-assisted trajectory."

Tarron clutched her hand. "Does that mean the danger is over?"

"It only changes the equation since this sun's gravity is involved."

Tarron stared at a monitor and sucked in a sharp breath. "The asteroid is going to hit the back thrusters!"

Jarill yelled, "Hang on."

The impact threw her out of the chair's restraints, ripping a scream from her throat. The ship spun out of control. Jarill smashed against a wall. Explosions reverberated in every bone like needled hammers. Blood dripped from the gash in her head. Her body clenched in hard knots as space swirled outside.

Monitors shattered overhead. Tendrils of red smoke curled toward the ceiling. Shrill alarms blared in defiance.

Tarron crashed against another wall. He shrieked—a sickening horror in his eyes.

Jarill's fingers clawed over the floor to reach him. Every muscle strained against the force pinning her against her will. One inch. Another. Sweat trickled down her neck like a wet spider. She maneuvered her body and slammed against Tarron. "Are you hurt?"

Anguish distorted his face. "Can't control . . . too many . . ."

"Tarron. Look at me."

He stared at her in glassy terror.

She could hardly think with the unceasing sirens screeching their warnings.

Horror shook Tarron's body. He screamed. "Agony . . . dying, dead . . ."

"Control your feelings."

His heartbeats thumped next to hers.

"Tarron. Listen to me. Stop feeling everyone."

His heart beat fast. Faster. Too fast.

She fought to pull back her fist, punched his face, and he passed out. She let out the breath she didn't know she was holding.

Every light in the room flashed off. The sirens stopped. Eerie silence hushed the room.

Jarill took a shaky breath, feeling safer in the darkness. Refusing to think of anything happening outside the room, she closed her eyes from the spinning of the ship and concentrated on the warmth of Tarron's body.

The whirling tore her thoughts away. Blackouts gave her welcomed relief until nausea wrenched her awake, choking her with dry heaves. During short terms of lucid consciousness, she hung onto Tarron. His steady heartbeat reassured her, and she kept repeating, "Please, let us survive. Please let us survive."

An eternity later, the ship lurched and stopped revolving. Lights glared on.

Jarill eyes dragged open in a squint of pain. She gently touched Tarron. "Wake up."

He grabbed his head and moaned. "I still feel . . . everything."

"This is not over."

Tarron grabbed his head and heaved himself off the floor. "You're hurt. There must be something here to clean your wound."

"I need to try the communication system." She stumbled up. Her hand trembled as she pushed in Maz's code.

"Is that you, Jarill?" Maz asked.

Jarill burst into tears. "You're alive."

"We're safe, Officer Ryz," Tarron said.

"Daz? Aronna?" Jarill asked.

"Without harm. I do not have information about your family, Sub-Ambassador Tarron."

"What happened to the asteroid?" Jarill asked.

"It left this solar system. There is too much damage to keep our ship in flight. Your daz is setting a course for the nearest habitable planet."

"When will we land?"

Maz paused. "We cannot land safely. Our ship is unable to complete the correct maneuvers."

"I'm coming up."

"There isn't time. I wish I could see you once more. May the stars give you life, Jarill."

The communicator sparked and died. Jarill stared at the panel in despair and slumped to the floor.

"We need to prepare for impact," Tarron said. "Help me."

Total exhaustion seeped into her body. "Why?"

"We survived the asteroid. We'll survive the crash."

Her heart couldn't contradict him.

"Help me find something to secure us," he said.

Jarill crept to the belts on the mangled chairs in the corner. "These are unsalvageable but the tungstonium hooks in the floor are intact."

She jerked open the doors under the broken monitors. Electric sparks shot everywhere. "Help me disconnect these cables."

"Looks dangerous."

"The shocks won't kill us."

"I'll do it," Tarron said. His hands jerked when he unscrewed two cables, but he didn't cry out.

Jarill secured them both to the tungstonium loops.

The spacecraft blazed through the solar system toward their obvious destination, a blue and green planet shimmering in sunlight. She didn't want to live there but knew the ship could never be rebuilt after a second collision without her planet's engineers.

"That is our new home," Tarron said.

"If we live."

"I prefer not to give up hope."

She gazed into his determined eyes. "I think I felt yours. Can you send hope to everyone on the ship?"

"I can try." He closed his eyes.

The spacecraft hurtled through the atmosphere.

She snatched Tarron's hand and held it tight.

"I love you," he said.

"Are you afraid we're going to die, or do you mean it?"

"I never lie."

A fountain of happiness spilled into her, overpowering her dread, if only for a second.

A great expanse of azure water and a small island of land filled a cracked monitor before the ship crashed into the ground with an ear-splitting blast. Thrown about, but secure in the cable, Jarill watched in terror.

The spacecraft veered sideways, shearing off mountainsides. It ripped through trees, somersaulted through the air, hit rock, and plunged, nose first, into the ground. Sand flew five-hundred feet into the air, filtering down to bury the ship and its crystal spokes.

Furniture collided over Jarill and Tarron. The lights wavered but stayed on. They grabbed their ears against the horrendous grinding of crystal and metal.

Complete silence scared Jarill more than anything. She and Tarron hung upside down, the floor now a wall. Spirals of red vapor slithered toward them.

"I think my hand is broken," Tarron said. "Can you release me?"

Jarill coughed, her throat raw. Blood hammered in her head. Every muscle screeched, refusing to move. She forced herself to untie her cable and dropped to a stack of jumbled tables. "We've got to get out before that vapor kills us."

Her fingers fumbled with Tarron's cable. "Are you in much pain?"

"I'm alive and thankful for that."

They pushed through the destruction and out the crumpled door into complete darkness. She looked back at the red vapor filling the room. One message faintly blinked on a monitor.

"*SURVIVAL RATE 4%, SURVIVOR RATE 4%, SURVIVAL RATE 4%.*"

Chills clawed down her neck. She sagged. "Only forty made it."

Tarron clung to Jarill. "Too much . . . can't."

She took his face in her hands. "You won't live if you can't shut them out. What do you do when you don't want to feel others?"

"Concentrate on intricate mathematical equations."

"Do that. Come on." She took out her crystal earring and lit their way across the jagged cracks in the metal floor.

"We need to find a doctor to treat our wounds," Tarron said.

Frustration and anger joined her growing panic. "We need to find famlezz and dig ourselves out before we run out of air."

"One task at a time. We'll find those still alive and hope there is an officer who can delegate authority."

She clutched the sharp ache in her chest. Tears dribbled down her face and she forced her mind away from thinking of her daz's bravery in the captain's chair at the front of the ship.

Tarron stuck his broken hand in a pocket and used one hand to climb up the distorted floor. "After we're organized, we'll gather supplies, equipment, and anything we'll need above ground to start a new life."

Her planet was gone, maybe her whole way of life destroyed. Somehow his words gave her unexpected comfort. She kissed his cheek. "You make me believe we can survive anything together."

PANDEMICS
By Ted Virts

"The US has a silent pig pandemic at its door once again"
                                            The Guardian 10/17/21

The warning came yesterday:
        a silent pig pandemic at our door . . . again

We didn't answer last time —
        Did we not hear?

Wilber has no word for his friend Charlotte and her web
There are no squeals of delight
There is no objection to porcine body shaming
They pig out in monastic meditation
Mud baths are silent

The march to market is stoic
Many morosely remain home
They just eat their roast beef
Or, tongue tied, have none
No cries of "wee, wee, wee"

Quiet cringing to the wolf's huffing and puffing
No pronouncements from the poke

They are smart, no doubt
Voluntarily drinking to excess,
        unable to comment to their drinking buddies
              human or snouted,
They only gesture at their truffle finds

We bring home the bacon
They have nothing to say.

A SOLITARY TEAR
By Mary Krakow

Night brings with it a certain intimacy.

Surrounded by family all evening, I alone remained. Mom was past the point of communicating, but her blue eyes fixed on me. A solitary tear tracked down her face.

I called to the nurse. "What does it mean?" The deathbed is a lonely, foreign place. I needed a guide.

"It could be, she's having a memory," she said softly, touching my arm.

Mom was propped in a hospital bed. Morphine kept her breathing shallow and steady, tricking her into thinking she wasn't dangerously short of breath. I gently brushed the tear away. Was she sad to leave this world she'd inhabited for ninety-five years? Her hand, usually cold, felt warm in mine.

I prayed she was pain-free, that the tear *was* the result of a memory, not a morphine-induced haze carrying her into the afterworld. She seemed alert and her eyes probed mine. We passed the night, our heads together, in a one-sided conversation where I tried to anticipate what she needed to hear. Even on her deathbed, Mom's concern for her children was palpable. I assured her I would look out for my siblings and that we would be okay. I held her gaze until the sun rose and her eyelids drooped.

Throughout the next day, family members gravitated to the nursing facility, speaking, holding her hand, stroking her fragile skin. By evening, Mom's breathing slowed until a final breath escaped her body and wrapped us in her grace.

A STABBING AT MIDNIGHT
A JONATHAN JONES MURDER MYSTERY
CHAPTER TWO: THE RETURN OF WINSTON

By Mike Cooper

With the body secured in the downstairs meat locker, the group returned to the dining room.

"What a ghastly turn of events," Marjorie Harmsworth said from the chaise longue. "I need a drink."

"It's seven in the morning, dear," her husband, Lucifer, responded from his station near the fireplace.

As Marjorie raised her middle finger, a fist pounded the enormous oak table in the center of the room and all eyes turned to Big Sam, the snake wrangler. "What we need," he said as they looked on, "is to figger out who killed Winny and string 'em up."

"Winston," said Lilith, Winston's wife—Winston's widow—who couldn't seem to stop rubbing her hands, as if she'd applied too much lotion and it just wouldn't absorb. "He prefers—preferred—to be called 'Winston.'"

"What you need," said a calm voice coming from the doorway, "is Jonathan Jones."

"How did you get in here?" said Persephone, Winston's younger sister, whose magenta beret was doing a poor job of hiding her inexpensive wig.

"I go where murder leads me," replied Jonathan Jones as he stepped into the light of the room. He was magnificent in a blinding white linen suit, his moustaches perfectly coiffed, tortoise shell glasses barely softening steel gray eyes that seemed to penetrate into one's very soul. He held an impeccable Panama hat in his hands, and there, on the middle finger of his right hand, was the signature ring.

"Are those real tortoise shell glasses?" asked Persephone.

"Why, yes," said Jones, his hand moving toward his face.

"Those must've cost a lot," said Lucifer enviously.

"Well, they—"

"Nice ring," said Marjorie Harmsworth.

"It's my signature." Jones gave a little flourish with his hand.

"Is that Panama hat from Panama?" asked Persephone.

"Enough about my impeccable taste. It seems there's been a murder," said Jonathan coolly as he surveyed the room.

"How'd you figure that out, Master Detective," said Persephone as she adjusted her beret and, with it, her wig, "was it the body?"

"Where do we keep the brandy?" asked Marjorie Harmsworth.

"Brandy is for after dinner, dear," her husband, Lucifer, responded. "What you want is vodka. Or sherry."

"No, no," Lilith said. "Sherry is for teatime."

"Sherry is for pussies," said Big Sam, still standing at the end of the table. "What you want is whiskey." He produced a battered copper flask from inside his pants. In another room, a cat yowled.

"May I see that?" asked Jonathan Jones as he swept gracefully across the room.

"Well, it's—" began Big Sam as Jonathan deftly snatched the flask, twisted the top, passed it under his world-renowned nose, and took a quick sip.

"Interesting," Jones said as he returned the flask to Big Sam. "Do I detect the bile of the Western Diamondback mixed in with your whiskey?"

"Puts hair on your chest," Big Sam replied.

Jonathan glanced down at his own chest briefly. "I see."

"What about my husband?" cried Lilith.

"My brother," said Persephone.

"Our acquaintance," said Lucifer.

"Can I get a hit of that?" said Marjorie to Big Sam.

Jonathan cleared his throat, which, from most people is a ghastly noise, but from Jonathan, sounded like an angel riding a Vespa. "We must first establish where everyone was at the time of the alleged murder. When was the last time each of you saw Winston alive?"

"I had a headache after dinner and went to bed early," Marjorie said.

"That was no headache," Persephone said. "You were four sheets to the wind. You kept singing 'Stairway to Heaven,' and you got the words wrong. It's 'buying,' not 'frying.'"

"And you?" Jonathan asked Persephone. "When did you see your brother last?"

"We had ice cream in the kitchen around midnight. Well, I had ice cream—fudge ripple. Winston prefers—preferred—raspberry sorbet," Persephone said.

"Even though you are lactose intolerant?" Jonathan insinuated, twisting the end of his moustache.

"How did you—"

"And you," he spoke to Lilith, "When did you see your husband last?"

"I'm not sure," she replied. "I'm an insomniac, so I took a sleeping pill around ten p.m. They had to wake me this morning when he—" She put her hands to her face and began sobbing.

"How convenient. And how about you, sir?" Jonathan spoke to Lucifer Harmsworth.

"I helped Lilith to bed around eleven," he replied.

"Carried," said Persephone.

"And you, Big Sam. When did you last see Winston?"

"Just now," said Big Sam. He raised his finger to point to the doorway.

Jonathan Jones's normally cool exterior flickered a bit as he turned to see a man standing in the doorway wrapped in several blankets.

"Winston!" cried Lilith as she rushed to the doorway.

"What the hell!?" Winston said. "Why did you put me in the meat locker?!"

"We thought you were dead, old sport," said Lucifer.

"I was asleep! Do you guys not know how to check for a pulse? Hold a mirror under someone's nose? For the love of Pete!"

"But the blood on your chest?" said Lilith as she wrapped her arms around Winston.

"I fell asleep with my sorbet! Are you all idiots?!"

"Well," said Big Jim, "I guess we don't need you here anymore, Mister Jones."

"On the contrary," said Jonathan Jones as he drew a silver-plated derringer from inside his vest and put two bullets squarely into Winston's chest. "Murder calls."

MOONFLOWERS
By Cameron Prow

My starshine stories await the moon to bloom.
Still
a few words escaping the time tether
help me hold on to the
hope of writing
what my heart needs to say
while I'm still here to say it.

OUR ROOTS
By Kimberly Bowker

The leaves turn color on a warm autumn afternoon as my mother swings the car into a graveyard in Ashland. This is not uncommon for us, to detour into a roadside cemetery somewhere in Oregon. My mother is the caretaker of our family history and we often find ourselves beneath the same mountains or on the edge of the same lakes where our ancestors once stood. She speaks their lives.

She drove my grandmother and myself to the tall grass swaying next to the curved headstones of William and Artinecia in the historic Jacksonville cemetery, nearly twenty miles away from Ashland. She once more gave voice to their story.

William's wife died on the first stop after the wagons rolled out of Independence, Missouri onto the Oregon Trail. She left her husband, a young daughter (Auletta, my great-great-great grandmother) and a newborn baby. The trio was accompanied by a cow whose milk fed the baby boy. The cow grazed on some poisonous weeds at Goose Lake, close to the family's destination off the Applegate Trail in southern Oregon, and upon drinking the contaminated milk the baby died. He is buried along the lake's shoreline.

It is said that Auletta lost half of a finger on the trail, an arrow pinning her smallest finger to the wagon's buckboard. My grandfather remembers looking at her hands when he was a child.

A love story unfolded on the trail, too. Before embarking from Illinois, Artinecia's husband died. She chose to continue the plan and drive the wagon with her young son behind her parents' wagon. She met William on the trail and after settling in the Rogue

Valley they had fourteen children. It is lost in history and time how they began their courtship, but I am sure the dirt remembers. Or the tress. Or the grass. Or the air. Or the sky.

One hundred miles north of Jacksonville, in Roseburg, my mother and I visit another cemetery. We see the crooked tree and the two small, rounded headstones that denote service in the Civil War on either side—there are my great-grandparents on my father's side, Martin and Anna. Yet another pair of great-grandparents on my mother's side, Olive and Gustaf, rest 160 miles across the southern Oregon landscape in a Klamath Falls cemetery.

During my mother and father's wedding at a family home in the Willamette Valley, my two great-grandmothers first met. Olive and Marjorie talked over appetizers following the ceremony and discovered that they grew up within an hour of each in southern Colorado. They are now buried within a few hundred miles of each other in southern Oregon.

Years down the road, my mother and I look at the fallen leaves on the flat headstones in the Ashland cemetery. We see the names of an additional set of great-great-grandparents who journeyed Maryland to Kentucky to Oregon—and I feel how I belong; I know my context. All our lives somehow intertwine, weaving into our roots, mingling with the trees and the air and the ground on which we exist. We stand with the past and listen about the generations of change that eventually becomes history. We intertwine. We grow into our roots.

PEONIES
By Ellen Waterston

Bouquet of living
song, pompoms
of gaudy reckless
bloom—what flagrant
petticoated pandemonium,
what lavish display
of unbounded giving.

Toss your pink mane.
Waft your fragrant jubilee.
Sing your refrain
of wishes for all
the madcap sweet good
to be . . .

even as loosed
petals kite high
and higher, riding
a sliver of zephyr,
before drifting downy
to the ground.

WOOD THRUSH

By Catherine Malcynsky

My father went by Melvin his entire life but now he goes by Mel. As he wilts, he responds best when you speak softly to him while pushing his wheelchair around. Such is his way when I visit him every Sunday, in the evenings, from four to six. Enough time to coax him into rolling a few bites of his dinner around in his mouth, enough time to help him into his pajamas before he remembers himself and growls that he's a grown man and can do the top button himself. It is not enough time to glean more than a few minutes with my father as I knew him, who breaks through in fleeting beams like the sun on a windy, overcast day.

As my father putters in and out of consciousness, our visits have become more frequent, and I find myself tracing my fingers over the flimsy spines of my memories, frantically searching for the stories only he can finish. Ever a man of few words, this has always been a delicate process—coaxing truths out of a long-repressed man. I don't know where our mother rushed off to when Allie and I were small, and by the time I could walk, Mel had fallen out with his brother, the shadowy Uncle Jack—and now there is no one else to ask about the broken branches of our family tree.

Six months ago, my father surrendered the little colonial on the edge of the forest and hasn't been Melvin since. After two years of Allie and I trying to hold his shaking hands, his final submission went more or less undiscussed—much like our mother's swift departure or the wine bottles that once populated our grandmother's trash cans. One morning he called Allie and grunted something into the phone, and by noon the two of us were on the front stoop with cardboard boxes and rolling suitcases. We packed up his paintings of robins and blue jays, helped him match his socks.

I didn't have time to count our growth spurts, marked in pencil along the kitchen doorframe. It didn't occur to me to unearth Allie's and my feather collection, still stowed away under the basement steps. In the guest bedroom, behind the frame of what was once my bed, I had scratched the initials of my first crush, S.G., into the molding. I'm sure the little letters were still there, under the bed skirt and a layer of dust, but I only thought of these things much later, after the realtor had found a bright-eyed family with an Irish setter and fresh blueprints for that little spread of land.

As we were closing up the truck, Mel kept asking Allie and me for things I'd never seen in that old colonial: his signed record of *What's Going On*; the photo of he and my mother at Cape May; the skull of the deer he'd shot up in New Hampshire—the size of an elk, he'd said.

Yes, I'd lied, *it's all here.* Only as the old colonial shrank away in the rearview, did I remember the Night Terrors I'd suffered there. I'd seen things, as a child in the dark; always things that could have been, but decidedly weren't—weasels worming around my sock drawer, flying squirrels swooping from arm to arm of my ceiling fan, owl eyes in my closet. My father capitalized and categorized them—Night Terrors, nothing more—and that was how we put them on the shelf. Even Allie wouldn't entertain their reality, lest these things scuttle about under her bed, too.

At the facility—a long, starchy building with buttercream walls—they gave him a room with a dresser, a bed, and a window. He'd asked for a desk, but they didn't have any in the basement. I asked why he needed it, and he said, indignantly, that he might want to make something. He'd never used the wooden desk in the garage of the old colonial; over the years, it had become a shelf for spare change, peculiar-shaped rocks, and old paint cans. But I touched up the varnish and brought it to the facility anyway. I doubt he will ever even slide out the chair.

For the most part, Mel alternates between his bed and his wheelchair, and when he stands he is never as tall as I remember him. His spine is curved like an old willow tree. When it rains we roam the hallways and he whistles bird songs, because he doesn't like to talk in public: the cedar waxwing, the prairie warbler. When I was a child I found this habit almost mystical, the way his tongue trilled against his lips, the roof of his mouth. I don't know if I can feel that way anymore, though I try.

As we wait for the automatic doors to part, I thank the nurses again for their time. Their smiles are warm in an electric-fireplace kind of way, turned on and off easily. On good days, in the evenings, while the sky hesitates to dim, Mel snaps his cinnamon gum and I swerve around the dips in the sidewalk. He taps his feet on the wheelchair's footrest as though he's walking himself, tiptoeing to some imperceptible rhythm. Sometimes he wants to speak to the canyon wren, and sometimes to me. In our native tongue we orbit conversations as we orbit the facility. The grounds are well-manicured and cruelly wide, a great pasture the elderly will never explore in this lifetime. It looks like the kind of space a horse would belong to, but there aren't any. Only the occasional squirrel makes a mad-dash across the vast expanse, feeling vitally exposed with every frantic leap.

I can feel Mel's body relax as we inch away from the buttercream walls, further into the air that smells of pine needles and damp earth. Ever a man of few words, he always saved his monologues for nature: talking to it, about it. The great Out There, he called it. The veins of the leaves, the ballads of the birds, the imprint of a rabbit's foot left in the garden. Because of him I am aware of my own chlorophyll.

Nature came for him, too, though. In the months before the facility, when he was still at the old colonial, he wasn't sleeping much. Night Terrors, perhaps, though he'd deny it. It was the branches against the windows, he said—like fingernails. Like the nails of the checkout lady at CVS, he'd said; those thick, bright acrylics that hooked at the ends. It sounded like the CVS lady was outside, scratching to get in.

So, we trimmed the tree. And things were better, for a while. But then the ants came. Little black ones, usually one at a time, on the nozzle of the tea kettle, or creeping up the side of his bedroom mirror. Mel was worried about their size, said the little ones never live alone. They don't wander far from their colony, and he just *knew* there were others—teeming masses behind the plaster, dutifully feeding the abdomen of their bloated, winged queen. So, he drilled a hole in the wall, to peer in, but it was too dark. He tore up a floorboard in the dining room, where he'd seen one scurry across the table. He set traps all over the floors, filled his cabinets with them. Allie called the exterminator, who said there wasn't a monomorphic soul anywhere on the premises.

I've found these talks at the facility to be the easiest I've ever had with my father, perhaps because of our orientation: much like when he used to push me on the swing-set, I stand behind him now, maintaining his momentum. The main difference, I suppose, is our trajectories: we are always moving forward, never backward. Spared each other's eye contact, which was always flickering at best, we speak instead to the great Out There.

I have to choose the right moment, like a berry from a branch, so as not to break the spell with something underripe and bitter. The small talk reminds Mel how to do this, how to hear a son and respond as a father, but I have found the lines he will not cross. I asked him once about my mother, how they'd met, and he sat there in his chair without a sound, lips squeezed together as if I might try and pry them apart. He wouldn't speak to me again until I came back the following week. Another time, a few weeks after, I asked if Uncle Jack was still alive, and Mel actually put his fingers in his ears, like Allie had when we were children and I talked about my Terrors. If the stories I ask for aren't in season with my aging father's disposition, he will start speaking to the birds again.

Tonight, the air outside the facility is now spiked with the smoke of a lone cigarette, but Mel seems in good spirits, nonetheless. The crickets, fewer in number than in June, shout to each other across the sea of green blades. I tell him about work, about the blueprints and the plans. I tell him about Mary, about the kids. Just when I think he may be listening, he says something about the swallows, how they shape-shift in the sky, and I can feel his body growing lighter in his chair.

Ahead of us, the sprawling lawn of the facility meets the tree line. I can't tell if what I'm seeing there are the fireflies, or if I'm blinking too fast. When I was young, all I wanted was to capture them, to fill a mason jar with a dozen shooting stars. My father didn't let me bring them in the house, insisting that they wouldn't make it through the night. He always made me let them go. Still, there was a thrill in that pursuit which could only take place in the night, and I caught them even if I couldn't keep them. I'd see a flicker just a few yards away, airborne and fleeting, and would lunge after it—but when I felt its little bug body against my palm, I inevitably screamed. It felt like the darkness was touching me back.

I stopped catching fireflies after I found the Still Girl in the woods. There are fault lines that certain experiences create, and from time to time they tremble. I know firmly that my father doesn't like it when I bring up the Still Girl. The morning after it happened, she became taboo: my father sat me down on the living room couch, took off each of my mud stained shoes, and I knew without asking that we were not to speak of the girl again. In the years that followed Allie would ask him, too—she had been staying with a friend, but had seen the news—yet Melvin would only tell us to leave it alone. *Just another Night Terror*, he said.

I know she is a forbidden recollection, but the evening feels suspended somehow, and I am not sure how many more chances I will get. I begin with, "do you remember," keeping my pace steady on the concrete. I wait for Mel to look over his shoulder at me, which he rarely does anymore. His eyes stay fixed on the coattails of the swooping swallows.

My heartbeat staggers as I broach the topic of that summer. I was seven years old. Or maybe it was September, and August was dragging her heels; it was still warm and I wore short-sleeve pajamas with bald eagles all over them. I had woken to the sound of Tilly pawing at the door, whining (she was still golden then, her muzzle not yet muted by the frost of old age), around what must have been three or four in the morning. When I opened the door I was holding her leash, but she took off, following her nose into the woods. She had never pulled me so hard before—in the dim lavender light of dawn my feet fumbled over roots and branches, sliding along the bed of pine needles, and at one point I fell and scraped the heels of my hands (those little injuries, the petty ones, they sting for so much longer, don't they, Mel?).

I called out for Tilly to stop—but by that point she already had, and I knew from a distance that something in the atmosphere had shifted. As I stood up, Tilly's voice jumped around her vocal cords, like she might actually speak to me. My pulse responded to the urgency of her whines, listening for those words, and I was suddenly aware of how alone I was. *Wake up!, Wake up!*, I thought, but I felt tragically certain of my consciousness this time.

Tilly was sniffing around something, her tail quivering with the vibrant emotion she couldn't articulate, and I walked toward her as though I might fall through the forest floor.

Speaking to Mel now, I frame my questions within the lapses of my own memory. I don't recall if Tilly first came upon the Still Girl's face or her feet, but I remember them both: her feet were small, like a ballerina's: only they were marble. Even the thick calluses on her soles had gone white. I can't remember what color her hair was, but I remember the way it was matted against the ground (like the clumps that gathered around Allie's shower drain). The girl's face had the same inanimation: still in a way I'd never seen features settle before, silent in a way that felt disruptive to the green all around her. I remember that her eyes were closed, but I felt like she could see me anyway. Her irises were veiled by her violet lids; her long lashes had gathered morning dew.

Tilly pawed the soil around the figure but didn't actually touch the girl. I remember wishing she would, so that I wouldn't have to. Even at seven years old I knew what was expected: that I would place my hands on her and wake her in some way, welcoming her back to the world . . . but the girl's cheeks were concave, sinking into her jaw. I didn't know yet what the word *emaciated* meant, but I've since attached her image to its syllables. Her clothes nearly blended into the ground, like they'd been chewed and spit out by the pines. There was something about her, even beyond her small frame, that cemented her in childhood just as it flung me from my adolescence. The finiteness of her stillness still echoes in my bones.

I don't remember going to my father, but I suppose that's what happened. I don't even think I had to ask my body to run. Melvin burst out with his binoculars, looked first to the branches out of habit. It was one of the last times I ever melted in front of him, and the last time he ever scooped me up. By the time the police arrived, morning had come and the heavens were weeping, and a nearby bird with a freckled chest had taken an elegy upon itself. For weeks after, Tilly would bolt to that spot every time we opened the door, and I would breathe a sigh of relief knowing that someone, however inhuman, remembered—until Melvin bought an electric fence.

I don't share this part with Mel as we near the end of the sidewalk, but if I close my eyes and breathe deeply, I can still smell the wet moss: thick and metallic. If I listen beyond the whirring of his wheelchair, I can hear the soft applauding of leaves in the rain. The questions the officers asked are lost to me now, but behind my lids I can see the lights sweeping across the soil, and the yellow tape that trembled with the weight of raindrops. In her wake, I wanted to know everything about the girl—but they wouldn't let me see her again. I saw the stretcher, the sheet pulled tight over her little frame, and I wondered what they would do for her inside that fluorescent ambulance.

I finish telling my father what I remember just as the shadows of the trees begin to lengthen. As twilight befalls us, I have to turn us back. The windows of the facility glow orange in front of us, and I can see a few figures parked in front of their respective panes, looking longingly at the great Out There. I tell Mel how he carried me out of the forest, dodging branches and roots. I tell him how he sat me on the couch, closed the curtains, took my shoes off.

I'm not sure if my father knows any more than I do about the Still Girl but talking about her out loud makes me certain that she was real; not just a Night Terror, like the creeping creatures and critters that had ransacked my childhood bedroom. I wonder if, like Tilly, the girl was buried in the shade of a gnarled oak tree.

If my father followed up with any of the officers, or unearthed any answers about the girl's brief existence, then perhaps Mel will tell me now, while it's still light out.

I ask him one more time: "Do you remember?"

I know she was a thief of his sleep, too—for weeks I'd heard the tea kettle whistle in the middle of the night. For the first time since I moved him here, I want to look at his face, map the places where it has eroded. When I look at him, I am reminded of the metronome below my own ribs, perhaps even more so than when I waited an eternity for the Still Girl's eyelashes to flutter.

"A wood thrush," he says softly. "She was beautiful."

DOES THE OCEAN LOVE ME?
By JoRene Byers

Does the ocean love me?
When I walk beside the foamy waves,
is she reaching out to me?
Is she sending tendrils of loving grace
with each endless surge?
Does she smile at me?
Does she want me to listen?
Have I listened well enough?

Does the juniper tree wait for me to greet it?
Does she give me a berry,
insisting I bite into the pungent
fresh resin?
Is she waiting for me to taste her?
Can I hear her loving words
in stillness and in the wind?

What lies beneath every quivering
aspect of these mighty gifts?
Is there ultimate love
in the sacrifice of a limb?
Does the ocean weep
when her children die?
Is that whale one of her beloved?
Does she grasp the last salmon
and miss their silvery sleekness
in her waters?

Does she long for the moon's gaze?

SERAPHIM
By Andrew Smiley

Deep within an ethereal plane that was neither Eden nor the World, a sprawling complex known as the Seraphim Organization kept watch over both spheres, recording humanity's narrative and intervening when it was necessary to ensure the balance between the Light and the Darkness stayed sure. The Organization was timeless—the intermediary between the Maker and its creations—but it changed its form and functions alongside humanity as it worked through the generations of its evolution. Guardians of their souls and final disposition, the beings populating Seraphim and its many branches and divisions stood ready to protect free will and agency of those living in both the fallen Paradise and the World it had given birth to.

The Director of the *Dea Familia* Eden Protectorate Program maintained an office deep within the Organization's administration cortex; close enough to the high heads of celestial governance to be well-informed but still functionally connected to the field agents and technology assets that she supervised.

Her name was Matriel, Director and Angel Imperator of *Dea Familia*. It was her duty to manage and organize the considerable stable of assets used by the Diet of Archangels and their servant Familias, and to handle operations where it was necessary to defend or protect humanity in Eden from the Darkness that threatened its future.

She was currently seated behind her wide, glossy conference desk, savoring a rare moment of quiet as the rest of the Organization pulsed with its perpetual cycle of activity around her. She was dressed professionally in a loose lavender blouse and narrow business skirt, a matching black jacket laid neatly over the arm of her chestnut-colored executive chair. A sleek pump dipped in a slow rhythm from the nyloned toes of one foot as she consulted several digital screens, drafting notes on a small personal tablet.

Behind her spread a wide expanse of white marble wall, streaked with bright veins of precious metals and rainbow tones created from the spiritual extraction of a vast spectrum of gemstones. The wall was dominated by an expansive diagram of Jacob's Ladder—the nine interlaced spheres that represented the celestial hierarchy of angelic beings—and traced by the descriptions of their orders, roles, and choirs in the various languages of Eden and the World. On the far wall facing her, a great six-winged seal of the Organization was wrought in gold, platinum, and silver along with its axiom: *"De Nobis Fabula Narratur."*

Thus, Their Story is Our Story.

On either side of the wings of Seraphim were 'windows' that displayed shifting scenes of places and times and events currently of importance or intrigue. Along the wall to the left of the Director's workspace hung a wide beautiful gallery painting of three exquisite trees whose roots were each entangled with the others; one with brilliant white foliage, one with green leaves, and one dressed in dark red. The rest of the wall space was dedicated to long screens filled with complex data and information streams bringing news and intelligence from across the districts of Seraphim's concerns.

Matriel was a woman of deep conviction and commitment, driven to give all of her energy and personal resource to the cause of protecting the souls of mankind from the elements of the Darkness set upon their destruction. Even now, while her surface thoughts were occupied with the bland narratives of the reports of a patron's Armory upgrade and the wording of an article of commission to a new set of young agents in transfer, the depths of her mind were still fastened firmly upon the grand scheme of the Organization's ultimate purpose. One smooth fingertip slowly traced the curvature of a letter of gold-dipped script etched into the desk's smoky quartz surface. She was ever aware of the seven Admonitions of the Covenant which every active Angel swore to when entering service in defense of those who lived upon the face of Eden. Nothing was more important to her than the preservation of choice and free will.

A soft chime sounded at her elbow, drawing her eyes to an incoming transmission waiting for reply. Recognizing the security encoding immediately, she nudged her devices to the side and opened the video call, sweeping up a few threads of dark hair back into her neat forelock and straightened her posture.

On the screen, a woman with steely gray eyes and black hair pulled back from a stoic, firm-featured face stared back at her. She sat in a posture of badly-concealed exhaustion, an arm draped loosely across one knee and shadows gathering beneath her bright eyes. Soft sounds of early evening trilled faintly over the audio channel, and low light seemed settled across the woman's shoulders, barely enough to show her subdued field gear and uniform in shades of black, gray, and midnight blue. In the lower left corner of the screen, an Organization identifier announced the caller: *Lady Sapientia, Noble Virtue of the Liminal Sphere – Acting Commander, Guardian Choir.*

"Director Matriel. I appreciate you taking a moment." The voice in the transmission was thin but carried the intensity and clarity of a hot copper wire.

Matriel smiled warmly, folding her hands over one knee. "Of course, Marshal. What can I do for you?"

"The situation in Brask is getting worse. More fey predators are infesting the woods, and the villagers don't have the means to defend themselves against nephilim of that type or number."

A solemn nod, and Matriel steepled her fingers below her chin. "Yes, I've been keeping my eyes on them, and the research Principalities supervising that region are becoming concerned lately; they've been quite a bit more . . . communicative than usual. Keeping Virgil—and two of my assistants—quite busy."

"They need help, and I cannot commit any of my forces to them, not when we are neck-deep in keeping these infernal Grigori bottled up in the mountain country." Sapientia's voice was heavy with distaste. "I need to call in an Angel interdiction from your division on their behalf."

The Director leaned forward, pulling her data wall controls near and turning to the long screen on the wall at her left, scanning the registry of active Familias and noting their current dispositions or mission flags. "I have two teams on standby; three available now—Sariel, Uriel, and Aladiah Familias." She considered for a moment, tiny lines appearing between her eyes. "I would recommend Uriel Familia's assets for the situation."

There was a visible pause from the Marshal's screen image, followed by a low sigh. *"Hm. Uriel's people."*

Matriel tipped her head to the side slightly. "You don't agree?"

"No objections, officially. But that Prelate, Nevitt . . . he is unruly. He reminds me of a wild dog that needs to be muzzled and neutered," came the Marshal's dry rejoinder.

"I understand," the Director made a conscious effort to hide her amusement at the statement, toggling information on the data wall until a row of five profile slides swept into place under Uriel Familia's digital seal. "Some of our Angels have more . . . *dynamic* personalities than others. Uriel Familia is very capable, and their

Covenant is untarnished. They have a broad skill set that would match the conditions evident in Brask."

A slow nod of agreement. *"I shall defer to your expertise, Matriel. You know them best."*

"Excellent. I'll begin drafting orders immediately." The Director swept up a platinum stylus and began pecking at command sequences on the complex logistics workstation to her left, several holographic windows opening in the static space around it. "You'll brief them in the field, then? The fewer filters, the better, as you often say."

Sapientia made a *tsk* of grudging acknowledgement. *"Yes. Though my window will be brief—there are several small operations to manage as we speak, and one of my lieutenants is succumbing to his injuries. I will not let him pass back into the Light alone."*

"Of course." Matriel softened her voice, her eyes meeting the Marshal's battle-hardened features as the silent whispers of a mutual understanding passed between them. *"In Caelo quies.* Your efforts and sacrifices are not in vain, Lady Virtue."

"Nor yours." The Marshal attempted a small smile. *"We all do what we must."*

Matriel busied herself with her devices, holographic windows opening and shifting around her workspace as she expertly navigated the multiple layers of clearance and security partitioning the Organization's functions. "I'll send them in. Magi Division will need your signet applied to the usual releases and requisitions; we can bypass the obligation phase since you will conduct their briefing on-site. While Uriel prepares his Armory, Virgil will secure their passage from the World, but getting them all notified and collected is a bit complex on a school day. Stand by for further updates—I'll have them to you within the hour, local time."

"Understood, Director. My thanks."

Sweeping a lock of hair back behind her ear, Matriel flicked over to a small window programmed with a name-generation algorithm. "This mission will be designated . . . 'Freewater.' Angels are on their way, Lady Virtue. You have my word."

"*Ad Astra per Aspera.*"

The Marshal of Zoar's image dissolved down into amber sparks as the transmission ended. The *Dea Familia* Director took a brief moment of pause, as she always did, closing her eyes and calling up the five young faces from the catalog of hundreds that she kept close in her thoughts. She reflected on the features of each one, reminding herself of the obligations they would carry into their mission—just another small but vital part of the struggle between the Light and the Darkness. Soon these children, both chosen by grand design and choosing to serve of their own volition, would plunge headlong into a realm equally familiar and fantastical to their inner selves.

It was time for her Angels to step back into their Glory and ride into battle once again.

LEPUS CALIFORNICUS

By Ginger Dehlinger
(after a traditional African American folk ballad)

Mr. Rabbit, Mr. Rabbit,
why are you called Jack?
'Twas jackass rabbit 'fore Twain cut it back
but I druther be Jacob, Johnny or Mack.

Mr. Rabbit, Mr. Rabbit,
where do wild hares roam?
Not too far from our sagebrush home
where the wind and the whip-poor-wills moan.

Mr. Rabbit, Mr. Rabbit,
what makes you run so fast?
Tall hind legs that help me outlast
coyotes and eagles that're after my ass.

Mr. Rabbit, Mr. Rabbit,
can you leap sky high?
Watch me fly, he said with a twinkle in his eye,
and with a flash of black tail, he bade me good-bye.

IF ONLY
By Ted Virts

My mom sits in her chair in the family room. She's stitching on a pair of embroidered pictures. One is a Raggedy Ann who finishes knitting herself. The other a Raggedy Andy pulling on a thread and unknitting himself. It is late afternoon. I start high school in the fall. My mom is captivated as the women's movement comes to magazines and television: *A woman without a man is like a fish without a bicycle. Does "he" really include you? All* men *are created equal.*

She keeps at her handiwork. She glances above the TV set to where the picture hangs—dark gray thunder clouds rising over a golden wheat field. I think it's dramatic and hopeful.

"Do you know what that painting is about?" she asks. "Rain before harvest will ruin the crop. Trouble is coming."

She confides in me a lot these days.

"Your father is drinking again."

"I don't know what to make for dinner."

"I feel like I could have been so much more."

She wonders out loud. "Is a woman's place in the kitchen? Is there something more important than being referee for you kids?"

"If only," she says. "If only things were different. If only you weren't here I could have done so much more."

I'm quiet. Do I make her sad? Do I disappoint her?

My sisters will be home soon. My dad will want dinner. We'll all sit down to eat. On good days we'll make fun of each other and laugh. On bad days, one of us will ridicule my mom and my dad will start yelling.

She teaches us to care about people. She reminds us—*Not everyone has it as good as you do* and *Don't let your smarts put others down.* The message: Be careful. Don't make people sad. Don't disappoint people. Don't make Mom cry.

"If only," she had said. "If only you weren't here."

If only you weren't here. So, I wasn't. High school was time away from home. I went to college at age eighteen. I never lived with my parents again.

My mom wanted the best for me. She told me that the world was there for me. She said that if I work hard I could succeed at anything. She would ask, "What do *you* want to be? What are *you* good at?"

I listened. Now, in my mid-seventies, I recognize that her voice led me to look out for others, to assume that the world held promise for me, and that "be careful" meant more than "be cautious."

I listened even though I heard things she may not have intended. She still whispers, "If only you weren't here." I wonder how it might have been for her if that were true. I wonder how it might have been for me if I had heard her differently.

My mom left me with two embroidered pictures. The doll that knits together, and the doll that unravels. They sit side by side.

INVITATION
By Carol Barrett

    i

Gold lace edged the card, 50th anniversary.
Surprised, I'd graced his third matrimony
a few years before. All three wives attended.
Grateful, said he couldn't make the gold
without their cumulative contributions.

Three cakes—chocolate, pistachio, almond
cream, a big 5 0 hanging from the deck.
He knew how to regale a crowd, raucous stories
running from guest to guest like loose dogs.
He even split the gifts. Joy all 'round.

    ii

Two days I watch a doe bearing down
in hot sun, first at my study window, then,
pains briefly halting, in the shade out back.
I pour water for her, offer apples.
Still she bellows, baby slow to come.

On the third day, neighbors coalesce,
several I've not met: a rehab doctor,
two nurses with blanket and gloves.
They'd heard her cries. We come together
for the deer, suffused with suffering.

iii

Taking a friend to chemo, I notice a basket
of hats, end of the line of chairs, near *Time*
and *Life*. Two left. Back home I gather the swarm
of kids lolling by on bicycles needing something
better to do. I hand out knitting needles, yarn

from the thrift shop, teach them to purl.
Hats appear on the porch like dahlias, orange
marmalade, purple, poppy red. Next trip to clinic,
I bring the basket, the blessings of young hands
soft and supple. Eyes follow me like bees.

LEARNING FROM BIRDS
A Novel Excerpt by Carolyn Tate

"Slowly, Margarita!" Don Ignacio admonished me in a whisper. "For a moment, keep it up, the foot, and slowly put it in front of you. Then, move forward with your weight."

I tried to balance on one foot and hover the other over the ground. This caused me to flap my arms and struggle to stifle my curses. Everyone else seemed to be able to walk this way. Ignacio and Alejandro were in front of me as we navigated the gaps in the netlike forest and poor Doña Dolores trailed behind me in the wake of the creatures my movements startled. Lift, hover, set down, shift. Try not to make noise. Silent jungle walking was at least as challenging as learning to dance the *cumbia* with Alejandro.

This was Learning from Birds 101. It was the first step of my new approach—to use the strategies of jungle creatures to counter the threats of Díaz-López, the archaeologist in charge of Pa'Witz, who was furious with me for trying to make a record of "his" ruins before the dam flooded the ancient city. What luck that Alejandro had introduced me to the guards' parents, Ignacio and Dolores, and that the student-teacher ratio was 1:3!

Two weeks previously, when Alejandro and Ignacio had discussed a birdwatching outing—no, a learning-from-birds outing, I kept trying to remember—Ignacio insisted that while Tonalá, where we lived, was excellent, a greater variety of birds lived around the remote Maya ruins of Pa'Witz, including spectacular macaws and toucans. After mulling it over for a day, Alejandro decided that he would take his first trip to Pa'Witz. He had it all worked out.

"If we go right after Easter, it won't interfere with my campaign. You can teach me about the history of Pa'Witz and how you work there. Once I understand exactly what's involved, I can inform tourists. We can go with Don Ignacio and he can show us the Maya way of birding. And I will meet the sons of Don Ignacio and Doña Dolores and discuss their issues with *el demonio.*" Everyone avoided saying Díaz-López' name.

Within ten days, we'd journeyed to the Usumacinta River and were negotiating the canoe to Pa'Witz. Once we were on the river, Alejandro couldn't contain his enthusiasm. He'd start to stand, then ease down on the bench, pointing this way and that. Above the din of the motor, he'd shout, "Look over there at ten o'clock. See the bird on that dead branch? That's an Amazon Kingfisher!" I'd turn to glimpse a flash of rich green wings exposing the orange chest and white belly of a bird that zipped along the river's edge then dove to snatch a fish. This went on; he spotted lots of parrots, some birds he called plovers, and he was really excited about a gangly crane hawk on the shore; apparently these are not so common in Chiapas.

To a non-jungle-dweller like me, the forest seemed menacing. I never knew which plants harbored fire ants or thorns, or which creatures to avoid, or whether to try to run from a jaguar. In my previous trips to study the ruins, I stayed near the cleared areas and hadn't really focused on the wildlife.

Once we arrived at Pa'Witz, Don Ignacio and Doña Dolores—I assumed she'd come to see her sons and nephews— received a big welcome from Mateo, Ángel, Juan, and Pedro. The elders shared the quarters allotted to the guards, where they had lived for years. Dolores used to make some money cooking for the trickle of tourists who ventured downriver. She immediately went to the stick-sided hut the guards used as a kitchen, presumably to assess any efforts that might be directed toward a meal.

Mateo walked with Alejandro and me to the *champa* where we were to hang our hammocks. In the shade of the thatch roof, he told me that Arqueólogo Búho, Díaz-López's assistant, had arrived by plane shortly after I left last time.

"Very ugly he was," Mateo said. "He knows you are staying in Tonalá. He says you have a bad reputation for being a criminal, for stealing from archaeological sites. He was very angry with us when we said you had not been here. He had a pistol, but he saw Juan pointing the shotgun from inside the block building. This made him more angry, but we do not tolerate people waving guns at us. He said we had to remember who paid us. He also said we had not been taking care of the buildings, but this is not true. He didn't even go into the ruins, so he did not know. Señorita, is very difficult for us, this struggle."

I looked at Alejandro, who had been listening. "I was afraid he'd come to find out why the attack failed."

Alejandro reacted quietly. He squatted and looked up at Mateo, who then squatted also. "Mateo, *h'mano*, you don't believe that Margarita is a criminal, do you?"

Mateo looked away from me.

"My family has known her for five years. She is a colleague of Doña Carlota, and Doña Carlota trusts Margarita with her house in Tonalá." Carlota had been photographing Maya sites for decades.

Dragging a finger in the dirt floor, Mateo shook his head sadly.

"You know my uncle Josue, don't you?" Alejandro asked.

"Of course, he comes with special tourists several times a year," Mateo replied. "Is very kind, Don Josue."

"My uncle, my father, and I met with Arqueólogo Búho in Tonalá. We told him we know that his boss wants to get rid of Margarita and we know that you men are struggling out here. We told him that if anything happens to her, or to you, we will know that he is the responsible one. We are on your side. He is the bad person, not Margarita."

"We know this, but . . . "

Rustling in the grass announced the arrival of Doña Dolores, who stepped up onto the *champa*'s raised dirt floor. The men stood when she entered. She and Mateo spoke in Yukatek for a few minutes. Several times she seemed to focus her eyes on a place that was out of sight. Then she hustled away.

"Come and eat, Señores, says my mother," Mateo's frown loosened its grip on his face and he nodded toward the guards' quarters.

I had never been inside the green-painted concrete block buildings at the site. This one had an opening that faced northeast toward the river, but as it was afternoon, the room was dim. We sat on benches on either side of a long wooden table. Dolores had produced some scrambled eggs, stretched out the black beans with some water, and was slipping tortillas off the griddle.

"Mmmmm . . . This looks very rich!" (In Spanish it's *riquísima*.) Figuring that we may as well eat them before some monkey stole them, I dashed over to the *champa* to get bananas and a papaya.

When I returned, only a few minutes later, the mood was much lighter. As I sliced the fruit, Don Ignacio and Doña Dolores smiled as they introduced Alejandro to their sons and nephews as "Don Alejandro Zavala Cordero, the manager of Hotel La Rinconada and sweetheart of Margarita." The guards then looked at me with surprise. I guess I had not mentioned a sweetheart. They always saw me with the different colleagues and friends who came to help me document the ruins. Who knows what conclusions they drew from my parade of guys.

Mateo asked what part of the site I was working on. I didn't want to mention the forbidden acropolis until I thought he might relent, so I told him about needing to study the birds.

"You want to study birds?" he asked incredulously. "Is this why my mother and father came? Tourists come from all over the world to watch birds here. We have so many, why didn't you notice them before?"

I started laughing. "Well, archaeologists are always looking down at potsherds and bits of sculpture and the ruins. Birdwatchers are always looking up. I never paid attention to birds, and they don't notice the ruins."

Juan the 49-er (he still wore this baseball cap) jumped up in the small space of the dining room and pantomimed a birdwatcher with binoculars, whispering gibberish as he walked smack into a chair, which prompted Pedro to imitate a tourist there to see the ruins, swatting bugs, wiping sweat, and trying to stop squirming long enough to take a picture.

After our *comida*, the guards, who were still on duty, returned to the ruins, continuing the endless task of keeping the jungle at bay. Before Alejandro and I left to go for a dip in the river, Ignacio said, "When the sun starts dropping behind the hills, I will take you to my spot in the forest. There we can observe the birds."

Late in the afternoon, Don Ignacio and Doña Dolores walked up to the *champa*. They led us from the bluff overlooking the river, where the modern buildings are, across the airstrip toward the forested hills. Where the cleared airstrip met the jungle, plants riotously took advantage of the abundant light from the clearing, creating a dense thicket. With machetes, Ignacio and Alejandro strategically sliced through the lianas, the vines that knit the forest. When cutting through the jungle, one tries to avoid causing the dead trees, whose descents had been arrested by these vines, to fall further and crush one's companions. At least that's what I hoped. After a few minutes of hearing me scrambling over or under the fallen trunks and grabbing the lianas in an attempt to slip through the slits, Ignacio decided I needed walking lessons.

"Slowly!" he whispered. "Let your foot feel where to go. Watch me." The way he moved was more smooth than bouncy. He kept turning his head, looking around, and took only a few steps at a time, stopping frequently. When he came to an obstacle, like a huge fallen tree, he managed to glide over it somehow.

Lift, hover, set down, shift weight. After a while, I could almost slither over the chest-high logs and feel into debris-clogged spaces. A tentative foot could test the stability of the surface and readjust, especially when steps were slow. This did give me more time to look through the network of the forest. Our shady path was occasionally stabbed by light flashing down the hill. It led us upward, gently, over the mosses and insects that crept on the fallen leaves, trunks, vines, roots, and rocks. We didn't walk long, maybe ten minutes, until we reached Don Ignacio's spot. A shaft of light descended from the west, partially illuminating a little alcove edged with rocks. On the downhill side was a tiny pond, or damp area, about a meter and a half across, around which there was lots of forest debris, but no birds.

Don Ignacio and Alejandro gazed up into the crisscrossing branches, not as dense here as they had been near the airstrip. Doña Dolores sat quietly on a large root of . . . I looked up and recognized . . . a ceiba trunk, stretching up into infinity. I backed away from the wet spot then tried not to move.

Alejandro appeared next to me. "When we entered the forest," he whispered, "the birds scattered. But they don't go very far. If we're still, they may come back." He found a rock several meters from the pond and inspected it for obvious critters before sitting on it. Ignacio and I did the same.

"The *selva* is alive with movements, small and large. But listen for the silences," Ignacio said quietly.

It's strange. I can distinguish between a hill and a pyramid covered with jungle. Fragments of pottery and obsidian leap out of the forest toward my eyes. But I just hadn't listened to the shuffling of fallen leaves disturbed by a lizard. There really is a lot going on. The breeze ruffles the leaves. Ants marching along their highway make tiny crackles. I could hear something dripping. Froggy burbles. Scratching. I closed my eyes and tried to hear the silences, but they were scarce.

"Use your eyes to scan," Alejandro whispered.

I tried, but seeing compromised my ability to hear.

After a while I heard a woodpecker thud-thud, thud-thud, thud-thud, on a tree behind us, up the hill. Another answered it from a different direction. This seemed to awaken the cenzontle, the local avian rock star, who sang a slightly different tune each time. Then, there in the thicket, on the other side of the pond, a large brown bird jumped from branch to branch, rather low to the ground. Another! Maybe a dozen! Suddenly a loud CHA-CHA-LAK repeated at rapid fire. The flock of brown birds flapped and glided in another direction.

"Chachalacas," Alejandro breathed. He had a little notepad and was writing something.

The noise level was picking up. YOINK, YO-INK YO-INK, sang some birds that looked like small turkeys tight-roping along the tentacles of a strangler fig. They stopped and picked at the tree, then kept stepping. A few climbed higher then started flapping their wings and YOINK-ing a lot. It was getting dark and harder to see.

Dolores and Ignacio stood and motioned that we should go back. We returned the way we came, lifting and hovering our feet over the logs and vines. When we got to the edge of the airstrip, the smell changed abruptly from gentle decay to mown grass. Above us swirled green parrots with red foreheads and red flashes on their wings. They seemed to be playing dive-bomb, flapping madly toward each other, squawking, then suddenly all flying in a formation, then breaking out.

We trudged in a more normal gait back to the *champa*. Alejandro pulled some Bohemia beers from the ice chest he'd brought and offered them around.

Don Ignacio accepted one; he and Doña Dolores sat on our log seats while we sat in our hammocks. "What did you learn from the birds today, Margarita?" he asked.

"Well, how to walk," I ventured.

"The birds showed you how quickly they can react to a noisy, fast-moving creature. They cried in alarm. Did you hear all the alarm calls when we entered the forest?"

I hadn't.

"A flock of *pa'ap*—jays—high in the trees started the alarm. Then the *panch-eel*, also nesting near the top of the canopy, cried 'petit pitit petit.' The birds alerted the *baats'*—the howler monkeys, who had been near us. They moved farther away and started to roar so they wouldn't cross into another troupe's range. Did you hear the howler troupes calling out?"

I had heard them, but I hadn't thought much about it. There are lots of howlers at Pa'Witz.

"These alarms, and others, caused the birds that had been quietly eating or working on their nests or keeping their eggs warm to fly up higher. This is your first lesson: the songbirds cooperate to protect one another from the raptors. They have different calls that communicate 'All is well!' or 'Where are you?' or 'Danger!' The *baats'* pay attention to the birds and so should you, if you are determined to work at Pa'Witz."

Alejandro climbed out of his hammock, washed his hands at our bowl-washstand and opened one of the food boxes. From a large bag he selected several items and placed them on a plate. "*Señores*, please have some of this *pan dulce* that we brought."

I stood too and poured Dolores some water in a small glass.

In the fifteen minutes since we had left the forest, the sky had darkened. It would be a moonless night. I lit a candle. It was mostly quiet, except for some distant howlers calling to each other. And some mosquitoes buzzing. We munched our bread.

"Listen!" hissed Don Ignacio.

"Urrrrrr! Urrrrrrr! Urrrrrrr!" A descending sound came from …

"*Xo'ch*," said Ignacio in Yukatek, then in Spanish, "*Búho*. It is time for the female to lay her eggs and he has found her several possible homes. He is watching over them while she decides."

"*Búho*. The screech owl," clarified Alejandro. "Like *el arqueólogo*'s assistant."

My throat constricted. Here I was at Pa'Witz, defying Díaz-López, and hopefully not endangering the guards. With Alejandro, without whose support I might not be alive, and with Dolores and Ignacio, who'd asked their sons to protect me. If I couldn't trust them, I couldn't trust anyone. It made me think of Little Blood, in the *Popol Vuh*. She was far more unfortunate than I; she had no one to trust. The owls were the servants of her evil father, One Death, but they helped her after all, pushing her through the hole that connected the Underworld to the earth surface. So, what did she do then, I wondered. Josue jokes that I'm reliving the story of Little Blood. I'm uncomfortable with that, I thought, but maybe, here, in this place where the Maya have lived for two thousand years, with these people who are trying to help me, I should open my heart to her story. Besides, I had the sense that I needed to be telling my story, not letting others tell it to me.

"If I make you some coffee, do you have time for me to tell a story from the *Popol Vuh*?" I asked everyone.

Ignacio nodded. "I remember the story that Don Enrique, the K'iché man, told us. It was about the Hero Twins and how they took the help of the animals to restore the head of Hun Hunahpu to its body in the Underworld ballcourt."

Doña Dolores looked at me intently without covering her face with her hands. That was unusual. She nodded, saying something in Yukatek.

As I fiddled with the Coleman stove and the cups and sugar, I decided I'd give the story some spin.

HAPPY BIRTHDAY
By Cameron Prow

The gift of your presence in my life is a treasure I cherish
I appreciate being able to talk with you about
the things that matter most.
Like a magic mirror,
you reflect new insights onto old truths.

I enjoy exploring the crazy world we call life,
especially the trails you and I have both walked
in tandem or side by side.

I don't know how I got so lucky as to have
a friend like you.
Each moment we have together is precious.

May your next year be filled with
courage to try new ways of
thinking
doing
being.

THE END OR THE BEGINNING
By Woody Medieros

Robert Fulghum, minister and author of *All I Really Need to Know I learned in Kindergarten*, said, " . . . all things live only if something else is cleared out of the path to make way. No death, no life; no exceptions." There is in life a beginning and an end; a first breath, a last breath; a contrast in existence. At least as we know it on Earth.

(1)

As you walk into the hospital room the nurse has just finished feeding her, cleaning her, diapering her—all things you told her you would never let happen. She has always shuddered at the indignities of her elderly bedridden friends. In a motion that has become automatic, you go to the corner and pull the old wooden rocker up to her bed. The nurse looks up. "Your grandmother is not doing well today," she says sadly. "She may not make it through the night." Your eyes tear and your throat thickens at the thought that tomorrow you may have no reason to come back, no one to come back to.

Sleeping much of the time, she lies curled in a fetal position; her shrunken muscles have grown weary and worn from age. Her cloud white hair is thin and sparse.

Closing your eyes, you try to picture her again with silver streaks in her thick, dark hair that she wore pulled back from her beautiful face. Even through the wrinkles, her face is still beautiful. You stroke her skin. It is paper thin, soft and delicate, stretched over the fragile bones of her small body. She has outlived most of her family and friends. Her life is behind her now . . .

she is dying. "A blessing," friends say, "she is so old." But it doesn't feel like a blessing to you, to be left with only memories. With tears of sadness, you hold her close for the last time. In fear of forgetting these last precious moments with her, you struggle to memorize her face, her feel, her smell, trying to burn them into your memory. Her eyes look up at you with childlike innocence, straining to focus on your face. No words pass. She is trying to pull you from her memory. You have been in her life for as long as you can remember, but she cannot place you.

"Will you always be here, Grandma?" you would ask her as a child. "Forever and forever . . . ," she would promise. Always the same question, always the same answer.

"Forever is not here yet, Grandma," you say softly to the bewildered face. You want to stop time—you want to hold her to her promise.

Startled, she opens her eyes wide. Struggling to sit up, she calls out a name from the past, a person long since dead. "Are you there, Papa?" she calls, her hand reaching out to her husband, gone so long now. Cold chills run down your spine as she stares past you, seeing something or someone you don't. Was he there now waiting to take her to the place beyond? You turn to look, half expecting to see your grandfather's ghostly form, almost smelling the leather of his old cowhide jacket; there is nothing there but an empty corner.

Gently, you take her outstretched hand. Attempting to imitate Papa's voice, you say, "Yes, Mama, I'm here." Smiling thinly, she lays back down and falls into a deep sleep, her tiny hand wrapped around yours. As evening comes, she slips away. Like the sands of an hourglass, her time of life has run out.

(2)

As you walk into the hospital room, the nurse has just finished feeding her, cleaning her, diapering her. You go to the corner and pull the old wooden rocker up to her bassinet. The nurse looks up. Smiling, she says, "Your granddaughter is doing so well; she'll be going home today."

Sleeping much of the time, she is curled in a fetal position, as if her tiny muscles have not yet adjusted from the womb. Her jet-black hair is thin and sparse. Closing your eyes, you try to picture her with a thick mane of dark hair like her mother. Her face is so beautiful! You stroke her skin. It is warm, soft, and supple, a little wrinkled, stretched over the fragile bones of her small body. She will have an abundance of family and friends, many of whom have not yet been born. "A blessing!" friends say. "She is so beautiful!"

"Oh yes!" you say. You know she is a blessing. You are excited at the prospect of the future. You can't wait to start making memories. With tears of joy, you hold her close for the first time. Smiling down at her, you try to memorize her face, her feel, her smell, afraid that you will forget these first precious moments with her, wanting to burn them into your memory. Her eyes, with a child's innocence, look up at you trying to focus on your face. No sounds pass. You know she is placing you in her memory. You are a special part of her life; she will remember who you are.

Startled, she opens her eyes wide, stretches and cries out. Is it something in the memory of birth that frightens her? Gently you rock her in your arms, "I will always be here . . . ," you say softly to the bewildered face of your newborn grandchild, " . . . forever and forever," you promise, and she will try to hold you to your promise.

As evening comes, she sleeps. Like a freshly turned hourglass, her time of life has just begun.

Does birth start only at the first breath, or does it also start at the last breath? A baby grows and thrives in the womb of her mother preparing for birth. Could it be that life on Mother Earth is a womb as well, where we grow and thrive, preparing for a birth of another kind? Does a baby feel, leaving the womb, the same as the dying feel leaving life?

That is something we will only know in the end or in the beginning...

CROWNING PIETY
By Carol Barrett

My grandmother never swore.
Not a hint of the *Heaven's to Betsy*
or *What in tarnation?* that tainted

the other side of the family—
Heavens to Murgatroyd, if things
got really tough. Easter morning

she poses, 1914, *Estelle*, for star,
a baby in her arms, rabbit ears
on the heads of two dozen ladies

from Fowler Presbyterian Church
in Sunday best, sleeves to elbows,
high lace circling the neck.

I bet she's thinking, *let's move
along, I need to get back
to my baby* (the word *nursing*, taboo)

then grade the last of my Albert's
student papers (half a point off
for each error,) *so he can prepare*

the next sermon from Revelation.
These floppy ears—she would
not even call them *a nuisance*

in private, not wishing to offend
a sister in the fold. After all,
one biblical woman with child

stands on the moon, wears a crown
of twelve stars. I wonder what
sworn testimony graced her lips?

THE ASCENT OF ACER
By Siobhan Sullivan

A maple tree seedling emerges from the soil, and leaves unfurl in shades of bright green. Diaphanous wings restrained by slender stems. They tremble together, trying to break free, but cannot escape. As time passes, the warmth of summer replaces the coolness of spring. The heat of the sun subdues and sedates the leaves. They forget their need to fly until one night, weeks later, spikes of frost collect along their edges. When they awaken, they are radiant with golden memories of summer. The days grow shorter, and a chill fills the air. One crisp morning, the leaves vibrate in a chorus of vibrant orange tones. Days later, layers of steel gray clouds collect overhead, filling the sky. A swirl of snowflakes drifts downward, landing on the leaves. They flutter and twist, turning crimson in their efforts to escape the icy crystals. Finally, they break free. The leaves fly together in a loose formation, rising and falling as one. Like dancers in the sky. They soar over treetops and skim over frozen waterways. And when the longed-for flight ends, they settle upon the frosty soil. The leaves turn russet brown and cover the forest floor with crackles and rustles. A savory scent marks the air at their passing. The confetti of their existence accumulates and creates rich, nurturing loam. Winged seeds helicopter over the forest, landing and anchoring themselves in the humus. A maple tree seedling emerges from the soil, and leaves unfurl in shades of bright green.

UNICORNO
By Ellen Waterston

Luis, he's the one in the white felt hat. Built like a fire plug.
Punches cows all week for wages,
then moonlights his rank bucking bulls at all-Mexican rodeos.
Like this one in Prairie City.

Ahead of the first bull, young men, black hair slicked, matching
purple satin shirts, slacks, and sashes, blast their brass trumpets,
stomp their silver studded boots. Paso Fino horses prance
on sheets of plywood, fetlocks combed and flowing, the
motionless riders extravagant gods in decorated sombreros,
fringed vests, and gaudy chaps.

Some kid named Levi or Shane or Clay from Molalla or Mitchell
or Terrebonne draws the one missing a horn. This bull's
reputation has invented a new form of dread. The rider climbs
on, too frightened to be afraid, pulls down his hat, grabs the bull
rope, figure eights a death wrap around his left wrist, across his
palm, raises his hand and nods.

The gate's flung wide. *Unicorno!* the announcer bellows. *Uno de
los toros insuperables de Luis Moreno!* Brute strength explodes out
of the chute, Unicorno's enormous head wagging, spittle flying.
The rider see-saws his spurs neck-to-belly along the heaving,
twisting gyre but is augered into the dirt in under four 43seconds.

If asked, Luis would tell you

his story

is not

the rider who hangs on for the full eight seconds, wins a belt buckle and some cash,

the speed bag boxer dancing in the shadows of the barn, staying quick and strong to make up for his small stature, the punching rhythm as even and sure as the bull rider's rocking spurs,

the macho man who hangs desiccated bull testicles above the door to his bedroom to ensure virility,

the rodeo clown who taunts Unicorno, dives inside a barrel, gets butted the length of the arena, then, when it's safe, climbs out to take a clown bow, one hand across his waist, the other generously gesturing to the crowd as if to say, "Don't forget, life's a cabaret, a roulette, brief, beautiful and strange."

No, Luis explains as he bites into a taco, chopped cabbage spilling on the arena's dirt floor. Mine is the story of Unicorno. I put my head down and go to work.

THE BEACH
By Joseph A. White Jr

Seagulls' cries mingled with the gentle swash and backwash of the waves. The taste of the salt air swirled in the light breeze. Kristin felt the warmth of the sun through her clothing. It was another splendid lunchtime stroll, just a short distance from her office at the bank.

She walked barefoot as she studied the random décor of broken crab shells, fractured sand dollars, seaweed, and water-varnished pebbles on the caramel colored sand. Suddenly, there was a blinding flash from the surface of the beach and her eyes shut tight. After a moment, with the afterimage fading, she looked for the source of the now-absent burst of light. Another small wave washed over her feet while her gaze swept the bubbles covering the sand.

So bright. What was that? Sifting the sand with her fingers; pushing aside pebbles in an ever widening arc, she found something and pulled it free. It was a necklace-pendant—a gleaming metal oyster half-shell over an inch long, but no chain. In its center, a generous sized, clear, faceted stone. "Is that a diamond?" she said aloud. Looking around, she was alone on the beach.

Kristen rinsed it, stood and held it high, turning it slowly. The sun reflected as before. She closed her hand over it. Time to return to work. Throughout the afternoon, the pendant sat on her desk, sparkling in the office lights as she answered emails and reviewed loan applications.

***

The electronic door-chime announced her entry into the jewelry store.

"Hi, Mr. Jenkins."

"Well, hello, Kristen. What brings you in?"

"I found this down on the beach today. Could you take a look at it, please?" She opened her hand and showed him her new found treasure.

"Oh my, that's a pretty little thing. What would you like to know?"

She handed it to him. "Is that silver and a diamond or just costume jewelry?"

He held it up to the light. "Let me check. I'll be right back." He tipped his head toward the back of his shop.

She watched him through the window in his workshop for a moment as he put the loupe to his eye and sat down. She browsed the display cases. When he returned, the pendant sat on a black velvet display board.

"I cleaned it and brushed a little sand from under the mounting. There's no tarnish."

"Oh, my," Kristen said. "It looks even prettier now. So much sparkle."

"It's not silver." He waited as she studied the item.

"Oh." Then, with disappointment in her voice, "It's just pot-metal?"

"On the contrary. There's a mark on the back, PT 999. It's platinum, the highest grade. That's very nice work."

"Platinum? Really?"

"Yes. And that *is* a diamond; an Ideal cut. I suspect it's over three carats. It's got great color and clarity. If you want a formal appraisal, say, for insurance purposes, I could arrange it."

Kristen looked at the jewelry, then at the jeweler. "Do you have any idea what it might be worth?" She looked at her prize again, dazzling under the bright lights.

"For a beachcomber's find, you did *very* well. Maybe as much as fifty-thousand."

Kristen's eyes widened. She sucked in her breath, and their eyes met. She put her hand over her mouth.

He waited a moment, then said, "To be sure, the diamond would have to be formally graded; the value of the metal can be calculated."

The only diamond she owned was her engagement ring, part of her wedding set abandoned in a jewelry box on the dresser in her apartment. It was the detritus of a failed marriage. Other shiny-brights she owned were on her cat's collar . . . a dozen rhinestones set in faux leather. She had some fashion jewelry—earrings and bracelets. Her salary was modest. She had worked her way up from cashier to loan officer at the branch in this sea-side hamlet.

Kristen said, "Someone must have been quite sad when she got home and discovered it was lost."

Mr. Jenkins smiled. "Maybe. But most probably furious at the inconvenience."

Kristen returned a puzzled look.

"Anyone who could afford a piece like that could afford to insure it. Aside from its sentimental value, she didn't lose much. When she got another one, I bet she bought a better chain." He chuckled as he picked it up and moved down to the next case, unlocked it, and took out a display of several silver chains. He selected one and slid it through the loop at the top of the pendant and handed it to her. "That has a sturdy double clasp."

Kristen looked at the price tag, then back at Mr. Jenkins. "Should I have it appraised?"

"Only if you plan to insure it. If you want that chain, it'll make a nice necklace. Even with that size diamond, the oyster shell mounting keeps it from being gauche."

"I'd like to think about it." She studied it a moment. "I really like it. Thank you for cleaning it. May I let you know in a couple of days?"

"Certainly. I'll keep the chain in the back for you." He reached under the counter and brought out a small white box lined with cotton, placed the pendant inside and handed it to her. She thanked him and wished him a goodnight.

***

As Kristin drove home from the jewelry store, her thoughts were on how she had not considered herself a lucky person, particularly because of the divorce. She and her husband had been excited when they discussed starting a family, but not long afterward he announced he had met someone else. Three months later, she was single. She dated a little but was careful; time was needed for the wound to heal.

So now, if the lucky little bauble was sold, what would she do with the windfall? Kristen wanted for nothing. Her car, although a five-year-old sedan, had low mileage, looked good, and was paid for. She had no interest in real estate, at least not yet. She had her health, friends, and the security of a good job. The pay was better than a teller but not as good as the bank's manager. But she could qualify to have her own branch someday because of the bachelor's degree from the college where she met her ex. Her life now, by any measure, was good.

Kristin purchased the chain and would wear the pendant, but not to show off. She wore it for good luck. It would be her talisman. She was grateful to walk on the beach whenever she wanted.

***

A few weeks later, a young widow sat across the desk from Kristen to discuss her mortgage loan application. Kristin noted the woman seemed anxious as she looked from the paperwork to Kristen's face and back again. The paperwork stated there was only one asset, a modest house owned free and clear. When her husband died, he had no life insurance except the mortgage insurance on their loan that had paid the mortgage debt in full.

Kristen looked up from the paperwork and said, "Mrs. Thompson, I received the appraisal. We loan up to eighty percent of the appraised value. What you applied for is right at the value of the property. We cannot meet your full request."

The woman shifted in her seat but said nothing as she now maintained eye contact and waited for the loan officer to continue.

"Your credit is satisfactory, but with this loan, your debt to income ratio would not allow the bank to approve the additional you requested on just your signature. Unless," she added, "you have some other source of income you haven't shown here." Kristen remained professionally detached from an applicant when she had to deliver a message like this. She waited for Mrs. Thompson to answer her implied question.

The woman's voice was soft as she maintained her gaze with Kristen. "No, no other income." Then she said, with confidence in her voice, "My job is secure, though. I *can* make the payments." She looked at Kristen, concern in her voice. "Could we still get the full amount the bank will allow . . . " Her voice trailed off. She lowered her head and began to wring her hands.

Kristen looked back at the application and turned to the next page. "I'm sure you would make the payments. There are guidelines, though, that must be followed." She looked over at the woman whose head was still lowered. Kristin thought, *Is she afraid the loan will be denied?* She had adequate income for her and her one dependent, a young daughter.

Kristen said evenly, "The space here for the purpose of the loan is blank." They could go no further unless that item was completed.

The woman looked up, started to speak, then paused.

Kristen had heard her share of what loan officers call, privately amongst themselves, hard-luck-stories. She had attended a class on how to resist a con job and knew how to prevent putting her financial institution, or her job, at risk; and how to refuse a loan without insult to the borrower. Refusing a loan was the most difficult part of loan counseling. Emotional burn-out for loan officers was one reason they left their jobs. Kristen waited for the woman to continue.

The woman's voice was subdued. "We have no health insurance. What we had was through Jake's employer and it was canceled when he died." She took a short breath, then said, "Gillian, my daughter, needs a kidney transplant. I'm a match and her donor. The tests were covered before his accident. But not the surgery." The woman stopped. She looked back down at her lap, then back to Kristin.

There was always a personal story behind each loan application. Kristen waited for the rest of this one.

After a moment, Mrs. Thompson went on. "I applied for new insurance, but there's a pre-existing condition exclusion. The regulations were supposed to have stopped those, but there's a loophole they used to refuse her coverage. I've tried everything.

My employer doesn't have health insurance; I earn too much to qualify for the state plan."

She maintained eye contact with Kristin. "In order to get her surgery scheduled, I have to guarantee the full amount for the surgery and post-surgery drugs for a year; that total is the amount I applied for. This loan is my only option." Her tone was matter-of-fact. Kristin did not sense a plea for pity.

Kristen now understood her customer's situation, felt compassion for her, and acknowledged her understanding with eye contact and a knowing nod. There was nothing in the woman's explanation that indicated she may be trying to game the system, and besides, the equity in the property would fully secure the debt.

Kristin opened the property appraisal folder and typed some figures into a spreadsheet on her computer. As she reviewed the results, she said, "Mrs. Thompson," then looked over at her. "May I call you Mary?"

Mary nodded.

"Mary, I estimated the net proceeds after a realtor's commission, other fees, and the taxes if you could sell the house for the appraised value. It's very close to the loan amount we could approve. So that wouldn't cover Gillian's surgery either."

"I know. I already talked to a real estate agent and she told me the same thing. She suggested I apply for this loan. It will be less disruptive for Gillian if we could stay in the house." After a long pause, Mary said, "The purpose of the loan is for my daughter's surgery."

"Okay." Kristen said. "I know you would like an answer as soon as possible. Our Branch Manager needs a day to review your application. Before I can send your file over to her, I need some additional information. Could you please provide a brief statement about Gillian's condition from her doctor and the paperwork that shows the financial requirements you have to meet? We'll need your income taxes for last year, with W-2s, and a recent payroll stub. I'll make a list for you." She looked at her calendar, then back to Mary. "Tomorrow's Tuesday and the loan committee meets on Thursdays. Can you bring all that in tomorrow?"

"Yes. Yes I can. You need all of that?"

Kristen nodded as she said, "Yes. What time does Gillian get out of school? Do you pick her up?"

"Yes. At three-thirty."

"That's perfect because I've got time to see you if you could come by at four o'clock. Would that work for you?"

"But I'll have Gillian with me."

With a warm smile as she stood to shake her client's hand, Kristen said, "That's fine. Bring her in. I'd like to meet her."

"Okay."

"Mary, I can make no promises, but I will make sure everything is in order for submission. I'll see you tomorrow."

***

Friday morning, Kristen left a message on Mary's voicemail that the loan had been approved. Could she come to the bank and sign the documents after three o'clock? The message ended with, "I'll be out of the bank this afternoon. Ask for Ms. Swanson. Have a good weekend."

When they got home, Mary fixed Gillian a snack and sat opposite her. She opened the manila envelope containing her copies of the loan papers, which included an envelope with the bank's return address on the upper-left corner in which was the deposit slip for her checking account that showed the deposited loan amount, eighty percent of the appraised value of their home.

Gillian had been watching her mother. "What's that, Mommy?"

"It's so we can get you your surgery, Honey."

There was another envelope, its corner just visible under the paperwork. It was a plain envelope, sealed, no return address, with only "Gillian" typed for an address. Mary held it up to the light. The security features would not betray its contents. She opened it. Inside was a single item, a cashier's check made out to Gillian Thompson— for the additional amount needed to cover her procedure.

Mary immediately compared the figures on the loan paperwork with the deposit slip. Those numbers matched. She searched through the pages. There was no documentation anywhere to explain the origin of the check. She stared at the check. With tears in her eyes, she looked at her daughter.

Gillian, with concern in her voice, said, "Is everything okay, Mommy?"

"Oh yes, Gilly. Oh yes. Everything's fine. Everything will be just fine."

***

Kristen took that Friday afternoon off to start her weekend with a long walk. Her bare feet were kissed by the waves as the water caressed the sand. There were voices of strangers nearby. She paused and gazed toward the horizon, the sun warm on her face. She smiled as she ran her fingers along the bare silver chain that hung loosely around her neck.

THE OBSTETRICIAN OF IRIS
By Ted Virts

Each morning
eager leaves stand
at attention
reaching for touch

when the light is right
              she approaches
      sensing
      assessing the promise
she offers
      a tender touch
      a kind caress
      a soft sigh

each day
hope-full
waiting
repeats

Until

the light is right
the blossom
the delight

YOUR SONG
By Amy Berlin

It's a peculiar feeling watching your father say "I do" to a woman who isn't your mother. It's a moment that will define the rest of you forever, the same way peeing in your pants in second grade will or your first French kiss. Something primal in my throat growled and I felt like eating my hand.

We're officially no longer a family. I wondered what my mother was doing right at this very moment, probably on mile eleven on her elliptical machine. *Skinny is its own prize*, she loved to say.

As soon as the bride and groom made their way down the altar I started my own processional to the bar. I was still pretty and just young enough to pull off flirting my way into an entire bottle of chardonnay from the bartender. I took it up to the venue's loft where I could avoid my father's sisters and cousins who acted like all of this was normal. Not even bothering with a glass, I gulped down the buttery liquid.

"Jeez and I thought I hated weddings," said a voice behind me.

I turned around to see a young girl, no older than thirteen, join me where I sat on the dirty carpet overlooking the dance floor. "What are you doing up here?" I asked.

"Isn't it obvious? The same thing you are."

Since I'd barely eaten all day the wine sloshed around in my stomach like a water balloon. I already felt the luxurious warm glow of tipsiness and it was as soothing as a bubble bath.

"Hey I know you! You starred as the flower girl," I said.

The girl framed her face like she was in Madonna's *Vogue* music video and then rolled her eyes.

"Excellent petal tossing, five stars."

"Don't you think I'm a little old for this crap?"

"I think you're a little young to be saying things like 'crap.'" I noticed her high top converse sneakers and chipped green nail polish on her stubby fingernails. "So how do you know the lucky couple?" I asked.

"Bride's my aunt. You?"

"Groom is my dad."

"I heard about you. Only daughter, parents married thirty years, mother is still fighting for alimony."

"Ouch. What an elegant hallmark card greeting."

"Hey, my parents divorced a year ago and now my dad is living with some hooker, so, I know the feeling."

"You shouldn't call other women 'hookers.'"

"Why not, that's what she is. She hunted my dad down like an antelope."

I considered this a moment. I had never thought to ask my father how he met his new wife. I knew from the Facebook photos that they behaved like they'd known each other longer than their six month courtship. I heard in my head the many midnight calls, me begging, *please let's be a family again*, him begging, *please don't you want me to be happy*. Suddenly I felt very stupid.

"Hey, your nose is bleeding," the girl said.

"Oh!" I pinched my nose and tilted my head back. The girl disappeared from view, her sneakers squeaking back down the stairs. A few moments later she returned and handed me a wad of toilet paper.

"Thanks," I mumbled. "My nose always bleeds when I'm stressed."

"What are you stressed about?" she asked. Her eyes were patient and calm like there was nowhere else she'd rather be.

I took another swig from my now warm wine. "My dad asked me to do a father-daughter dance with him. It's hard for me to participate in this new family funhouse."

"So, don't do it," she said.

"It doesn't work like that."

"Why not? Seems like you're trying a lot harder than him."

"You don't even know him," I said. The girl offered a small shrug. "What's your name, anyway?"

"Victoria."

"You don't seem like a Victoria. A Vicky maybe?"

She pantomimed barfing. "I hate it, my parents have a thing for old lady names. My little sister is named Eugenia."

A shift in the downstairs music caught my attention. The song the DJ was playing faded to a murmur and then Elton John's "Your Song" came on. That was my cue. The wine in my stomach gurgled its way up and gnawed at my throat. I slugged down some more and stood up, watching my father search for me in the crowd. The song was only two verses in and I saw him reach instead for Jessica, his new wife's daughter, only a year older than me but with shinier, butterscotch colored hair. He twirled her and gave a heedless *it's my wedding day* smile.

My body slurped back down to the floor like a loose ramen noodle. I let out an involuntary yelp. I wished I could dissolve into the stained carpet; this was definitely more humiliating than peeing your pants. I watched as they shimmied their way across the dance floor while family and friends clapped and adored them. As if the hundreds of times we danced together like this in front of our big brick fireplace was just a dress rehearsal, and now today, it was the performance he was always meant to give.

I'm not important sprouted like a swallowed peach pit in my stomach.

I felt Victoria's hand perch on my shoulder, its heft offering the comfort of a grandmother. Looking over at her, my face hot and sticky, I said, "am I still bleeding?"

PARK BENCH
By Ted Virts

Jesus sits on the park bench.
He looks at fall colors,
        splendid this year,
and feels at one with the universe.
He does that a lot.

I walk up.

"Can I join you?"
        "Sure, of course," he says.
"What should I call you?"
        "'J' is just fine, " he says.
"That's my brother's name."
        "I know," he says.

I sit.
I say,
"Do you mind a few questions?"
        "If you must. I don't mind. Really."

"Thanks.
> I'm not sure of what to think about you.
>> Son of God?
>> Judge of heaven and earth?
>> Wizard?
>> Brother?
>> Friend?"

"Just call me 'J,'" he says.

"So, what am I to do?
> Worship?
> Keep kosher?
> Kill the infidel?
> Hope things are OK now
>> between your dad and us?
> I'm confused," I say.

Jesus looks at me.
He says,
> "I love these fall colors.
> Don't you think they're beautiful?"

CANADIAN LAB, EH?
By Suzanne Merrick

The morning after we got Tucker was a blur.

I actually slept pretty well once I'd finally been able to stop FREAKING OUT about what I'd just done. Buying a puppy from the creepy guy across the street? REALLY?!? $200?? Where in the world did I come up with that amount?? Did I have $200 in my bank account? What would that guy do if I bounce my check for the dog??

DARN! He probably would have sold him for $50.00. Shit. Now I have a dog I know nothing about and I've committed to something I really can't afford to do.

The kids spend every other weekend with their dad and his twenty-seven-year-old girlfriend. Our twenty-seven-year-old receptionist, to be exact. I'm a forty-year-old, almost-divorced, single mom, trying to sell real estate in the middle of a recession. What was I thinking?? Actually, I know the answer to that question. I wasn't thinking. All I saw were my two amazing kids smiling at me. Smiles that I would give anything for these days. SHOOT! The kids will be pissed if the guy takes his dog back because I've bounced my check. Charley will give me THAT look. UGHHH!

Opening my eyes, I roll over to the edge of my bed and look down to see Charley sleeping, taking up her entire dog bed. Tucker's curled up on the hardwood floor next to my girl with his chin on her back. Looking around the room, I'm pleasantly surprised to see that there are no messes in my bedroom. No obvious "markings." No dog toys ripped up. No half eaten shoes. My bedroom furniture intact. Hmmm, maybe this puppy's going to be just as perfect and sweet as Charley after all. An entire pot of coffee later, I call the Vet and make an appointment to take the puppy in.

Charley's always somehow been able to decipher when she's getting into the car to go to the Vet versus getting into the car to go to the river. Even when I pretend we're going to go do something fun, she always knows! Since being diagnosed with a Thyroid problem, she's been poked and prodded so much that I usually have to carry-drag her through the door of the Vet's office. Once inside the waiting room, she squeezes as much of herself as possible under the bench. I suppose she thinks that if she can't see the Vet, the Vet can't see her!

Recently she completely refused to get out of the car altogether. Charley did her best Jell-O impression. Lifting her out of the car, she wiggled out of my arms and hopped into the third row of seats, then went limp. Charley weighs about 100 pounds, but in this moment she felt like a 300-pound dog. There was no way I could lift her over the second row of seats. I walked back into the office. "Charley's refusing to get out of the car." The Vet Tech laughed. She and the Vet ended up doing Charley's exam in the back of my car that day.

Preparing myself for a difficult time at the Vet's office with Tucker, I down another cup of coffee. "C'mon Charley, we're going to the Vet." She gives me a panicked look. "I'm pretty sure he's never been in a car before. He's been following you around, doing everything you do. If you get in the car, he will too." On top of the fact that I've just told her where we're going, I remember Charley's "Super Power" of mysteriously knowing when we're going to the Vet. Great. I'm gonna need more coffee.

Surprisingly enough, she seems uncharacteristically at ease. I notice her give Tucker THAT look. We've all seen it. It's the look an older sister gives her annoying, naive little brother when she knows something bad's going to happen to him but she's elated it's not her in the hot seat.

My VW Bug's easier for Charley to get in and out of and there's no third row of seats to deal with, so I decide to take that car. Charley quickly hops into the back, laying in the middle of the seat, leaving little room for Tucker. Fortunately, Tucker doesn't seem to mind and happily curls himself into a tiny ball on the floorboard behind my seat. Great, I think. Tucker's going to be just as easy as Charley. I can't believe I had any doubts.

Pulling into the parking lot of the Vet's office, Charley groans as Tucker jumps onto the small portion of the backseat that Charley isn't occupying and also onto a large portion of her hind quarters. Instinctively, Charley's Super Power kicks in . . . she spreads herself out on the backseat, making herself as heavy and as large as possible. My 300-pound Golden Retriever. Obvious relief in her eyes as I put her leash on Tucker, not on her.

Tucker hops out of the car excited to see what this next adventure will entail. Prancing across the parking lot. Ears flopping, tail wagging high. Everything in this new world's so fun and sooo exciting! As the other dogs, cats, ferrets (and one snake) in the waiting room watch Tucker and I approach the door to the Vet's office, I'm sure they're all surprised to see Tucker's enthusiasm about being there.

I've barely opened the door and he noses it the rest of the way open, announcing his presence in the waiting room. Immediately he makes intimate friends with the gentleman's crotch just to the left of the door. As I'm shutting the front door, I hear the gentleman's cat in the cat carrier on the half wall behind me hiss loudly.

Turning around, I find Tucker now aggressively sniffing an older Cocker Spaniel who's with an elderly lady with pink hair, outfitted entirely in purple. Until we arrived, it appeared that they were sitting quietly next to the gentleman with the great smelling crotch. The Cocker Spaniel ducks under his owner's legs.

A Great Dane next to them stands up to see who's causing all the commotion. Tucker gets this "GAME ON" look in his eyes and begins to taunt the Great Dane in the middle of the tiny, crowded waiting room.

A young boy with two ferrets, sitting next to the young pregnant lady with the Great Dane, has a panicked look on his face. He puts the ferret cage behind him. The pregnant lady becomes extremely concerned upon realizing that her normally mellow Great Dane is out of control and that she's incapable of helping this situation.

A HUGE tattooed man seated next to ferret boy has two cats in separate cat carriers. He puts them both on his lap and holds tight.

Tucker's only five months old and probably no more than forty pounds, but I have to say, he's holding his own with that full-grown Great Dane in the waiting room. In between sparring with the Great Dane, he's making sure everyone's included in this amazing fun. Great smelling crotch guy, ferret boy, tattoo-cat man, pink haired lady, pregnant Great Dane Mom.

I'm trying to reel him in, but the leash keeps getting wrapped around everyone's legs. My mind's racing. In between apologizing to everyone, I'm yelling commands. "TUCKER!!" "COME!" "STAY!" "SIT!" "LEAVE IT!" "HOW ABOUT A TREAT??" It's no use. He doesn't know his name or any of the words that make Charley stop dead in her tracks. The receptionist stands up. "Suzanne, we have a room for you now." Gosh, I feel bad about taking cuts. On the other hand, I think everyone's very relieved to have all THAT fun come to an end!

Once in the room of our own, Tucker calms down... slightly. There's just sooo many smells. And that treat jar on the counter. "It's so high up. I might have to jump on that counter to get the jar ... but then how do I open that thing?" Tucker's in his own world, now consumed with new adventures and smells.

The receptionist hands me a clipboard with a pile of paperwork to fill out. Name, phone number, address, email address, age of dog, breed of dog... I'm trying to remember last night. As I was leaving the creepy guy's house, I turned back. "Oh, what kind of dog is he? And how old is he??" Laughing he said, "His birthday is November 25th, the day before Thanksgiving. And, hahaha, he's a REALLY RARE Canadian Lab, worth thousands!" Okay. I remember. November 25th. Canadian Lab.

Upon entering our room, Tucker inspects the Vet's crotch with force. She tries to make small talk. Gives him a treat. Asks about Charley. Gives him a treat. Asks how I came to be the proud new owner of such a boisterous man. Gives him a treat. I have to say, she is most amazing Veterinarian! She takes his temperature as he's getting a treat and he's absolutely delighted in it! As she does his entire exam, Tucker seems totally happy with everything.

Flipping through the paperwork I'd just filled out, she starts to snicker. "Uh, Suzanne, Uh, Canadian Lab? Hehe. Where did you get that? Hahaha." I give her a puzzled look. "Oh, well, the guy I got him from said he's a Canadian Lab." The Vet laughs even harder. "He's most likely a Wirehaired Pointer/ Lab mix. HAHA... Sorry... HA. HA. HAA! Does he say 'EH' after every bark? CANADIAN LAB!?! HAHAHA!!!" Stupid Vet. Just as I suspected, the visit wasn't cheap, but she said he's healthy, so that's a relief.

Walking Charley and Tucker around the neighborhood tonight, two ladies approach us. "Your puppy is so cute! He's a Canadian Lab, right?" "He certainly is," I replied. "A REALLY RARE Canadian Lab."

LIVE LIKE SOMEONE LEFT THE GATE OPEN - SIGN FROM HOBBY LOBBY

It's been a few months since Tucker adopted us. I'm feeling pretty confident that we've found another dog just like Charley. He has come into our lives just when we needed him, and I'm 100% certain he's going to be just as perfect as Charley—once we get through the puppy stage. He's growing like a weed and has sooo much energy. I'm sure my sweet girl was the same way when she was a puppy but I've just forgotten.

Instead of doing our normal route around my growing Northwest Crossing neighborhood, I've begun taking Tucker and Charley to area dog parks. Charley's getting older and doesn't like going for long walks anymore. Short walks leave Tucker with lots of excess energy. The dog parks are a great solution for both dogs.

Charley doesn't really care about the dogs at the park, but instead makes her rounds to all the people, making sure everyone's gotten the opportunity to pet her.

Tucker, on the other hand, runs and runs and runs. Then runs some more. The more dogs who chase him the better.

After Charley's made her rounds, she comes over, sits by my feet, and gives me THE LOOK. "Okay, I'm ready to go now. Let's get our dog and leave." Tucker usually does a few more laps. Eyes glistening, ears flopping, tongue hanging out the side of his mouth, tail high. A look of total elation. As he finally slows down enough for me to grab his collar, I attach the leash. On the last few fly-bys, Charley looks up at me and rolls her eyes as if saying "UGHH! THAT DOG!?!"

Embarrassing to admit, my time at the dog park has become the main socializing event of my day. I love talking to the dog owners. I love seeing all the dog's different personalities. Plus, I've discovered that dog parks are absolutely fantastic people watching places. Really. When we go to the dog park at a particularly busy time of day, I hang around the perimeter and see how many people I can correctly match with their dogs. Kind of like my own made-up version of "Dog Park Concentration."

Have you ever noticed that it's usually the biggest, most tattooed man, dressed in all black leather, in the middle of summer, who comes into the dog park with the toy poodle in a plaid sweater on a blingy leash? Or the two tiny little old ladies who bring their gigantic Great Dane named Maximillion to the dog park? True story. Max is actually one of Tucker's favorite dogs to play with. When those two dogs run by, the ground shakes and it literally sounds like two horses running by. The ladies yell to everyone standing close to where Max and Tucker are headed—"DON'T LOCK YOUR KNEES!"

The day the ladies (they're sisters actually—super cute gals!) adopted Max, they brought him to the dog park along with an older, smaller dog and that's when we met. Like most dogs, immediately upon going through the gate of the dog park, they head to the farthest corner of the park and do their business in the hardest to reach spot. Max was no different. Max's newly adopted moms look to each other for a bag to go pick it up with. They both pull snack sized ziplock baggies from their jacket pockets. I laugh and hand them one of the bags I'd collected from the poop bag dispenser just outside the gate. Then looking at the size of Max, I hand them two more. Just in case.

On the other side of town running errands with Tuck, I spur-of-the-momently decide to try the Big Sky Dog Park where we've never been before. As usual, there's the normal "greeters" at the gate. They all seem to be nice enthusiastic dogs like my boy, so we enter. Tucker immediately takes off running, continually looking back to see how many fun dogs are chasing him. I scan the park for a quick lay of the land. Nice, bigger than our neighborhood park. Kind of a different mix than at our local dog park. That's cool. Tucker's already being chased by a couple of Labs, some sort of Cattle Dog and a Doberman who's obviously older, as after the first lap, she sits down and just barks loudly as Tucker runs by.

Out the corner of my eye, I notice a couple who are probably in their fifties, placing their toothless Long-Haired Dachshund on the top of the picnic table. Cute. I'd never seen a Long-Haired Dachshund before. What a cute dog! WAIT. There's a PICNIC TABLE in the middle of the dog park! Gross. I certainly hope nobody comes to the dog park for a picnic. I can only imagine what's happened on the top of that table! After seeing an elderly man sit down on the one bench inside our dog park and immediately get peed on by three different dogs, each one marking his leg over the other, I quickly learned it's safest to stay standing and keep moving around at all times when at the dog park.

Oh! Someone new is coming into the dog park. The greeters ascend onto the gate. This time it's a twenty-something in jeans and a t-shirt. One tennis ball in hand, he's being followed by his small Bulldog. He's either a brave guy or very inexperienced at dog parks. Everyone knows that you never walk in with a pocket full of treats and that you never, ever just bring one tennis ball into the dog park. He must be a newbie. This should be fun to watch.

Tucker, still happily being chased by a group of dogs, is oblivious to the new addition to the dog park crowd.

The twenty-something throws the tennis ball across the field where all the dogs are playing. His Bulldog takes off like a shot, uber focused on the tennis ball. Even though the ball being thrown catches the interest of a few other dogs in the park and they attempt to run after it, the Bulldog is lightning fast and gets to it well before any other dog. He brings it back and drops it at his owner's feet.

The twenty-something throws it again. Again, the Bulldog speeds past all the other dogs and brings it back. I'm completely in awe. I've never seen any Bulldog move at that speed, and so focused. Wow.

The twenty-something throws the ball one more time. The Bulldog races full speed ahead towards the tennis ball. He's completely focused on the ball and doesn't notice Tucker heading into his path. Turning back to see how many dogs are chasing him, Tucker collides into the Bulldog. The Bulldog does a sort of tuck-and-roll maneuver and just as it looks like he's about to pop up and continue on his path to get the ball, Tucker trips and slams the Bulldog back onto the ground. Finally getting to his feet, Tucky shakes it off and gives me a look of "What the HELL just happened? WOW. THAT was SUPER FUN!!" The Bulldog jumps up as Tucker rolls off of him. Looking Tucker straight in the eye, he growls, snaps at my boy, then turns away and runs after his ball.

Looking around to see if anyone else has witnessed this, I notice that most of the people at the park are on their phones tonight and not paying any attention to the hilarious situations happening around them . . . this one in particular. That is one of the funniest things I've ever seen! I'm giggling hysterically about all of this . . . to myself, mind you . . . like some crazy lady. SHIT. I see an elderly man smiling at me a few feet away. "Is that your dog?" He asks. "The funny one who doesn't seem to care about anything but having fun? Boy! Don't you wish we could all live our lives like that?"

NEW MOON, BELOVED DARKNESS
By JoRene Byers

This is the elegant time
of perfumed thoughts,
when dreams are sent into the ethers
and the sky rains down starlight
to kiss the eyelids of devotees
everywhere.
Fragrant ginger and nutmeg
warm the fire of possibility.
A wish may be fulfilled and singing heard again.
The tea leaves whisper of
sirens and firelight.
The moon grows now,
as my dreams take root
to flourish
and nourish,
and become real to the touch.
This is the bounty of the moon,
the roots setting forth
so the tendrils
can grow into the light,
the light that loves
unendingly.

JUST ENJOY
By V. Mello

Just enjoy the sun, for one day we won't see,
Its rays, heat our face as masks are permanently
Mandated, ever since we rose 5 degrees C,
Now the wars for food and water are constantly
In the 2020s, we lived with no real fear,
Scientists, the Nobel's, they'll figure it out in the near
Children are aware of our approaching planet's doom,
Industrious adults couldn't fathom losing Zoom.

Just enjoy the ocean, for one day we won't see,
It's blue winds race and caress our face, as our masks are permanently,
Required, so hot without them, we can't even breathe,
Now the wars for food and water is our anarchy,
We snatched and pulled trillions of fish,
So much by-catch, that's us fulfilling every wish
We can and we will, continue it's plunder,
For man, it knows little of wonder or surrender.

Just enjoy the food, for one day we won't eat,
All the insects have died, no soil, just heat.
Most enslaved, since we rose 5 degrees C,
Now the wars for food and water, in perpetuity,
We thought we were separate from the Earth,
We thought we could control and command Her dirt,
All the magic she offered to all and for free,
We spent carefree, O how these egos breed.

Just enjoy the Moon, for one day we won't see,
The waves to surf our soul as masks a permanently,
Needed, ever since we rose 5 degrees C,
Heeded never, now a heated decree
The top 1% live on Mars and the other planets,
We saved 1 species, while destroying all other inhabitants
Was it worth the sacrifice to save this human race?
Let's roll the dice, and see how we treat the rest of space.

BEWILDERMENT
By Krayna Castelbaum

For Lucky, canine companion, in memoriam
(August 2003 – May 2019).

When finally I surrendered
all effort to fathom

how we can love beyond measure
what cannot last –

my heart rolled, a child at play
in newly mown grass,

rolled and rolled in green promise
upon a sea of crimson petals

fragrant with the lush scent
of spring peonies

MORNEY
By Kathryn Mattingly

I've come to Italy to nurse my wounds, having lost another child and knowing it will be my last attempt to bear children. My doctor and friend, Grant, tells me that it takes more courage sometimes to give up and accept fate, than to try and change it. He's lent me his late aunt's house here in Rome, near the *Piazza Navonna*, to help heal my frazzled nerves, which have made me painfully thin. Each morning after a sleepless night I carelessly tie my blonde hair in a ponytail, throw on my jeans and a sweater, and sit at this outdoor café in the Piazza.

I silently pray the late April sun will warm my numb heart as I sip on a cappuccino and think about the children I will never have. I cry behind my sunglasses and wipe away tears before they can escape down my cheeks. On my third day of this ritual that does not soothe my agony, a young gypsy appears out of nowhere. I think surely she is an angel, with eyes as dark and deep as God's richest earth and curls the color of mahogany bark. She peers up at me while holding an enormous white cat in her arms.

"Have you some change?" she asks.

Her English is decent, and I find myself charmed by her confidence. The round eyes stare at me innocently. A little red tam on her head matches the plaid woolen skirt she wears. I think she looks more like a porcelain doll than a beggar, for her skin is pale and undernourished.

"I do have change," I tell her, "but why don't you sit with me a minute and talk?"

Her dark eyes look puzzled as she nervously pets the cat.

"I'll buy you some milk, if you'll just sit for a while," I plead.

After a glance in each direction, she sits down, and the cat lets out a mournful meow. It jumps from her arms and crouches under the metal chair. The gypsy child doesn't appear at all concerned that her cat will bolt. And it doesn't. The feline begins to lick its paws contentedly.

"What's your name?" I ask boldly.

"Morney," the gypsy angel says.

"Is that Italian?" I inquire.

"No. My mama is American. Her mama was a Morney, until she married Grandpapa. I think Mama misses them, her family in America."

I ache for her soul that is wise beyond its years.

"Is that why you speak English?" I ask.

"Yes, Papa does not speak it."

A waiter appears, and I order milk for my little friend. The waiter looks skeptical, with one brow arched. I look him straight in the eye, even though he can't see my eyes behind the dark shades. He nods and leaves quietly.

"Well, it's a beautiful name. Where did you get that big fluffy cat?" I sip the cappuccino, never taking my eyes from her thin, angelic face.

"She *is* fluffy, isn't she?" Morney swells with pride for her enormous feline friend. "I find her one day, making screechy noises. Poor thing . . . so tiny, and starving." Not unlike this child before me, I think to myself, as she turns her head of tangled curls and points toward the cobbled street behind us. "There, in the side street. That's where she was. Papa let me keep her." Morney looks at me, her eyes serious. "But now he says she is too big and eats too much and I must take Chintzy to the cat place."

"The cat place?" I ask, amazed.

"Yes, in the ruins, where Caesar died. It's not far from here."

"Why do they call it the cat place?"

"Because there are many, many cats. Maybe a hundred." Morney reaches under her seat and pets Chintzy while the waiter places a glass of milk in front of the child and disappears, not a smile or a word crossing his lips. After one gulp, she stares at the saucer beneath my cup. I offer it to her, and she pours the milk into it carefully, placing it in front of the beloved pet. Morney is kneeling beside the chair, and I smile at her red knee socks and little loafers. Someone has mindfully kept this enticing lure for pity from becoming too shabby.

Every day she comes, holding her large white cat, all the while stretching her hands out from beneath the feline to receive coins. The rich tourists at the cafés along the Piazza ignore her and I marvel at how they can be so complacent. Who could resist giving change to this brave little spirit, a mere ghost of a child, with dark shimmering eyes and messy curls beneath a red tam? I find her scrappy courage contagious, and somehow the pain of my loss is less suffocating. After nearly two weeks of this daily ritual with the child and the cat and the milk, the gypsy angel comes on a warm sultry morning without Chintzy.

"Papa took her to the cat place," she moans sadly. "He says she drank the little bit of milk we had for my sister Lydia." The stoic child hardens her eyes rather than cry. "I will visit Chintzy, every day maybe."

"I'm so sorry, Morney," I mutter, thinking how often I have heard these words myself, and not found them helpful.

"I hate begging!" Morney announces. "But if I do not beg, then Lydia will have no milk, even though the milk is made bad with the drugs." Her tone is sharp with anger.

"Lydia has drugs in her milk?" I ask, bewildered.

"Yes, it is to make her sleep, so Mama and Papa can beg, and she will not cry. I wish," she confides in me, "one day to have many coins, so many, I never will beg again. Then Lydia can have milk that is not drugged, and she can be like other babies, shopping with their mamas."

I nod, unsure of how to respond. "Perhaps one day, Morney, you will grow up and earn money in one of the shops where you see the mothers with their babies."

"Perhaps," she replies, and leaves hurriedly without touching her milk.

One day Morney brings her baby sister in a carriage that is tattered and worn. She asks me to care for Lydia because her mother is too ill to beg and her father has not returned from the bars. Nervously I look about and see not a soul taking any notice of this battered pram housing a dark-haired darling like her sister. Hesitantly and with many misgivings I concede and tell Morney I will watch Lydia while sipping my cappuccino, but she must return for her by midmorning. As my little gypsy friend runs off into the cobbled side street of the Piazza, I see a woman looking sickly and frail, and well beyond her years, looming in the distance. I wonder if she is Morney and Lydia's mother.

Amidst odd and perplexed looks of pedestrians strolling by and café waiters gawking at my table, I study the little one placed in my care. She never opens her eyes fringed with curled lashes. Lydia's face is round and smooth like Morney's, another cherub with mahogany hair, and I wonder if her eyes are as dark as her sister's. When no one comes for her, I reluctantly stroll the sleeping Lydia across the Piazza and ask about her family in the shops. In one store on the corner of the narrow-cobbled street someone knows her parents. The shopkeeper tells me the father and mother have probably run off, because the father is wanted for killing a man in a bar brawl.

"Roberto is a violent one, when he has been drinking." The little man uses heavily accented English. "He and that woman Isabella are like shadows of the night, always working the back streets."

The shopkeeper tells me he hopes they will pay for the crime, having shamelessly overdosed their young daughter, addicted to the drugs almost since birth. I anxiously peer down at Lydia, but she is waking up from her drug-induced sleep. I can't help myself as I reach for her, to cradle the toddler in my arms. She is so light I wonder what there is of her beneath the shabby blanket.

The storekeeper stares painfully at the baby and tells me it will also die from the drugs in the milk, which are too strong. "Roberto and his woman have less sense than most." He shakes his head sadly. "They are so young, and the mother . . . she takes the drugs. But Roberto . . . he is just a thief and a drunk."

"What do you mean, she will also die?" I ask, looking at him puzzled and confused. "Is this not the child you feared was overdosed? See . . . she is fine!"

"No. Not that one, not yet anyway. The other one, with the cat."

"*Morney?*" I whisper, staring helplessly into his bushy-browed eyes.

"Yes, that's her name . . . Morney. She is dead a year this . . . this month I think."

"But how can that be?" My mind races backward. I remember the pale woman in the shadows, the blank stares of the waiters and their non-recognition of my little gypsy friend, who has visited me every day for two weeks, begging coins while stealing my heart. I remember Grant telling me I hallucinate because I am not well—

the drugs, the tests, the pregnancies, the lost babies, the strain of it all. He insisted I must take a long vacation. And now this, discovering Morney has died, well before she could have brought me her sister Lydia this morning.

I decide to leave Rome. I will reside in Milan. There is nothing to return to the States for. Unsuccessful pregnancies have taken their toll on my marriage. Before I go, I visit the cat place Morney spoke of. It is indeed a refuge of partially restored ancient ruins, right in the middle of the city, one story beneath ground level. The whole area is over-run with cats of every size and shape. The felines vary widely from fat and sassy to haggard and frail. A big white cat sits like a queen among them, and it is Chintzy. I am sure of it. Dusk is settling in, and the lights play tricks, but I swear that in the shadows I see Morney, in her red tam and plaid skirt, waving at me. She is kneeling by the huge white cat, stroking its soft arched back with her free hand.

Racing down the cement steps with her sister still in my arms, I shout out *Morney* but only the cats respond, with wild guttural meows. Sitting down on a large stone in the ruins, there among the whining, growling cats, I cry into Lydia's mahogany curls. We sit for hours in the darkness, huddled together for warmth, but Morney never reappears.

At home now in Milan not a day goes by I don't think of the little ghost-child and her huge white feline. But thankfully, the voices and illusions within me have not come again. And I have a daughter who needs me, since her father was imprisoned for life, and her mother is dead of malnutrition, or perhaps a drug overdose. No one could be sure. But I am sure of one thing. It was Morney who brought me Lydia, an orphaned gypsy no more, but a child of my own at last.

WIDOW'S WALK
By Ellen Waterston

She ghosts into the harbor. The day—cold, moleskin gray. The bay—
all hers, emptied of yachts waiting out winter on cradles in
the shuttered boatyard.

A high-sided, regal sloop, this one. Her gunmetal gray hull mimics
the water's inky hue. How neatly she slices through the waves. No harbor
jumper, she, no day-tripper.

Lithe, elegant, this slender queen is rigged for going—self-winding
winches,
roller furling, go-ashore dinghy inverted amidships. There's no question
she's headed for blue water adventures too broad a reach for me now.

With my glass I spy the skipper, cloaked in a billowing black poncho,
materialize
like a specter from below, lower the tender into the slate water, row to
the town wharf
then back, climb out with a grocery sack.

That night and the next no stern or masthead running lights. No sign of
light or life at all. Pitch on black, like the great blue heron that disappears
silently into the dark. Whoever it is seems happy to be alone, a skill I've
never known.

I've grown attached to this solo sailor, try and try to read the sleek sloop's name, home port, but the harbor breeze stays northerly. Her stern is never to me. How I want to stow away, maybe then I'd find out what is and isn't out of my question now.

But the next day I can but wave as she weighs anchor, motors as far as the first bell,
then jubilantly raises Genoa and main. A downwind fills her wing-on-wings of brilliant white,
speeds her away, leaving me to claim

what's left of what I came for, when my sails more full, when not even the sky was a limit, when I just knew every question had an answer. It's three years to the day you died. It's not out
of the question the ghost ship spirited you back to remind that time and tide wait for no one.

MY UTERUS IS IN THE FRIDGE, AND OTHER STORIES

By Niki Rainwater

There is something poetic about the pathology building's location, adjacent to the beauty college. Maybe it's the painkillers talking. Two men standing outside stop their conversation to watch as we pull into a front row parking space. "Civilian" visitors are not a common occurrence, it seems.

"Can I help you?" one of the men asks as he opens the main entrance door. "Yes," I answer, almost giddily, from behind a mandatory surgical mask, "I'm here to pick up my uterus." I've been waiting a week to say this out loud. I even practiced in the car. My adult son grins. I search the man's face for . . . shock? Disgust? Joviality? Instead, the man pauses, and with a thoughtfulness I wasn't expecting, says, "I'll go get just the right person to help with that." He then disappears behind a pair of stainless steel doors. A lifetime total of three careers and seventeen jobs, I've been "just the right person" exactly twice. And I've just quit one of those. My kindergarten class and my womb, gone in the same week.

"They think I'm nuts, don't they?" I ask my son, who dutifully answers, "Of course not, Mom." That grin again. My no-nonsense, medical-minded daughter called ahead to arrange the pick up while I sat beside her on the porch, abdomen cradled in pillows.

A cheerful, young woman emerges from the double doors carrying a small manilla envelope. "Does this happen often?" I ask her. "People coming in to reclaim their organs?"

"Oh, you'd be surprised," she says. We both laugh. She hands me a clipboard to sign, then looks for my approval before handing my son the envelope. "My first home," he says, receiving the package with tenderness. A whip-quick sense of humor is only one of a million things I love about my children.

"Are you ok, Mom?" my son asks from the driver's seat.

"I'm ok, Honey."

My uterus is hermetically sealed in plastic. We examine it closely, with fascination and wonder. It looks like something you might find in a kosher deli.

"My uterus is in the fridge," I say aloud at every opportunity. I mean, how often does a woman get to say this? The phrase amuses my liberal and conservative friends equally; my eighty-seven-year-old father too, and that *is* saying something.

A hot, August Saturday finds my teacher colleagues setting up their classrooms. I enter mine, pack up my things and say good-bye. Today is a good day for a burial.

I place clipped greenery inside the soft, deep bed my son has dug in the lawn. I hold the pouch to my heart and weep. I pour my uterus into the earth and thank her for carrying two remarkable humans to safety, and for the two she could not. We cover her with a blanket of flowers culled from gifted bouquets.

The sun rests but a moment on the horizon and sighs. My tears become nectar for the hummingbirds.

COWG ANTHOLOGY CONTRIBUTORS

Carol Barrett directs the Creative Writing Program for doctoral students at Union Institute & University and has taught poetry at COCC and Saybrook University. Her books are *Calling in the Bones* (Snyder Prize, Ashland Poetry Press), *Drawing Lessons*, and *Pansies* (creative nonfiction finalist, 2020 Oregon Book Awards).

Amy Berlin is a positive person who writes depressing fiction and poetry. She has no credentials, has not yet been published in a literary journal, and keeps writing anyway. Amy is currently working on a short story collection—spoiler alert: it does not contain happy endings.

Kimberly Bowker is a writer based in Central Oregon. She is the organizer of *Central Oregon Book Project* and has written for various local and national publications. She loves to explore how everything connects.

JoRene Byers is besotted with roses, tea in lovely teacups, and books. She keeps company with the mountains nearby and all the mourning doves, quail, and jackrabbits that visit daily. She resides on the traditional homeland of the Wasq'u (Wasco), Tana'ma (Warm Springs), and Numu (Paiute) people.

Krayna Castelbaum publishes *Poem of the Month* and collaborates with other creatives in Central Oregon and beyond. She also instigates monthly Poetry and Bookmaking Playshops that free people to invest energy in creative exploration and self-expression. She's at work on a collection of poetry based on *The Sopranos.*

Barbara Cole, PhD, has owned her own testing and training company and taught management throughout China, Ecuador, Kazakhstan, and Pakistan. Her work has appeared in *Still Point Arts Quarterly* and *Woods Reader,* among other. She divides her time between Monterey, California. and San Miguel de Allende, Mexico.

Retired from a career in academia, **David Cook** now writes poems and short stories about the real world and fiction, often from an unexpected perspective. He tends to probe the present and the future with a touch of irony and humor.

Mike Cooper holds an MFA from Oregon State University-Cascades. He is president of the Central Oregon Writers Guild and teaches writing at Central Oregon Community College and Oregon State University-Cascades, as well as creative writing workshops through Blank Pages Workshops and The Forge.

Seetharam Dravida is a retired professional. He is a lifelong learner with a passion for reading and writing. He loves to travel, meet new people, and hear their stories. "A Date With the Hirwas" is his first story.

Ginger Dehlinger has self-published two novels (*Brute Heart, Never Done*) and a children's book (*The Goose Girl's New Ribbon*). Her poetry has appeared in over a dozen journals and anthologies, and her short story "Francine" was first runner-up in *The Saturday Evening Post* Great American Fiction contest 2022.

Jennifer Delahunty is a Sisters-based writer whose work has appeared in *The New York Times, Blue Mesa Review, Bend Magazine,* and *Fourth Genre,* among others. She has taught at the University of Arizona, where she earned her MFA, and at Kenyon College, where she also served as Dean of Admissions.

Robin Emerson lives in Bend, Oregon. She recently contributed a story about speech recovery to *Just Say "Yes" to Life: Stories of Thriving After Stroke.* She is a long time student of aikido and trains at the Oregon Ki Society Bend Dojo.

Ted Haynes is the author of six books set in Central Oregon—most recently *Pole Pedal Murder,* the fourth novel in his Northwest Murder Mystery series. He is a founding board member of the Waterston Prize for Desert Writing. Ted and his wife, Joan, live on the Little Deschutes River. www.tedhaynes.com

Mary Krakow is a retired educator. A member of COWG, SCBWI, and E-Z Writers Critique group, she writes flash fiction, children's fiction, and letters to her elected officials. Mary's work has been published in various anthologies, as well as in print and online sites. Visit her blog for writers at www.findyourwritingnerd.com.

Dr. MJ Kuhar grew up in Western Pennsylvania. After medical school, she completed an obstetrics/gynecology residency and a one-year fellowship in reproductive endocrinology. "In Vitro" is her first novel, which she hopes will soon be published. MJ lives in Central Oregon and volunteers for organizations dedicated to improving children's lives.

Denice Hughes Lewis is an award-winning e-book, self-published author, and screenwriter who specializes in fantasy and sci-fi. She's also a freelance editor currently critiquing writers at the Palm Springs Writers Guild in California for their monthly contests.

Catherine Malcynsky's stories have appeared in *The Susquehanna Apprentice, Broad River Review, Carve Magazine,* and *The Masters Review* Winter Story Award shortlist in 2020. She is currently a writing instructor at Oregon State University-Cascades, where she enjoys good books and bad puns.

Kathryn Mattingly is the author of fiction novels *Benjamin, Journey, Olivia's Ghost, The Tutor,* and *Katya. Fractured Hearts* is the title of her short story collection. Kat has won several awards for her fiction. She enjoys mentoring new writers while teaching novel and short story writing at her local college.

Woody Medeiros has lived in Old Town Bend, with her husband Dennis, for over forty years. She has four children, seven grandchildren, and, coming soon, great-grandchildren. Woody retired in 2020 after a long and wonderful career as Director of Grandma's House of CO, a shelter for at risk young mothers and babies.

V. Mello is originally from NYC and now living in Bend. He has been influenced by hip-hop and rap. He primarily performs spoken word, which is motivated by current and historical events along with his lived experiences in nature.

Heading to college, **Suzanne Merrick**'s kids made her pinky-promise to not become a "Crazy Dog Lady." She absolutely kept that promise. She didn't adopt 100 dogs. Or dress her dogs up (except for holidays). She went on dates…with Tucker's approval.

Eric Moser lives in Terrebonne, Oregon. He worked for the US government, most recently the US Forest Service for thirty-two years as a hydrologist. He's long considered himself a writer with boxes of manuscripts to prove it. "A Time to Die" is his first piece to be published.

Gerry Pare and her six siblings were raised by frugal parents of French and Ukrainian descent on a small Oregon farm. Her present novel involves a teen cellist, time travel, and Niccolò Paganini. She resides in Talent with her husband, a bassist, surrounded by pear orchards and pot grows.

Cameron Prow's creative endeavors have earned first place finishes for Poetry (2012) and Memoir (2013) and third place for Fiction (2014, 2020). Her poetry and prose have been published locally and regionally. Cameron's hobbies include reading, jigsaw puzzles, and building family from friends one heart at a time.

Niki Rainwater, Bend resident of seventeen years, is the author of recently published children's story *Rosie Rides the River*. Her writing is inspired by her travels through rural Asia, Europe, and North America. Among the publications her work has appeared in are *Northwest Crossing Living* and Copperfield's Books' The Dickens.

Gerald Reponen graduated from the University of Minnesota. He became an Air Force pilot, flying photo reconnaissance. After four tours in Vietnam, he wrote *The Vietnam War: My Life in the Air* *and on the Ground*. After age eighty, he has written thirty books on his life experiences for family.

Lynda Sather lived and played all over Alaska while managing public relations for the Fairbanks school district and Alyeska Pipeline Service Company. Now retired, she splits her time between Fairbanks and Central Oregon, aka Alaska Lite. She is thankful to the Central Oregon Writers Guild for encouraging and supporting her writing addiction.

Jake Sheaffer found his love for the craft of writing in the summer of 2009 while in Durango, Colorado. His first foray was with screenplays but transitioned to literature when he fell in love with adjectives and how they can inflate, embellish, or amplify a character's clothing or how snow accumulates. He is drawn to contemporary short stories and science fiction that explore wonder and fear.

Andrew J Smiley is a middle school Language Arts teacher and has been a resident of Central Oregon for the last decade with his wife and three children. When he is not trying to save worlds through the written word, he can be found watching anime, playing video games, exploring dark corners, and tinkering with Gunpla models.

One summer morning at age twenty-one, **Scott Stewart** hitchhiked to Oregon from Southern California and knew immediately he was home. He's lived in Eugene and Portland, recently retired from a career in state and local government, and resides in Bend, near his daughter, granddaughter, and son-in-law. He writes fiction.

Lyrical language, combined with scientific facts, highlights **Siobhan Sullivan**'s work. She is working on novels for children set in Oregon's High Desert. Siobhan shares nature, history, and cultural experiences in her blog, *Bend Branches,* and in the High Desert Museum's volunteer newsletter. She enjoys blending words with photographs and artwork.

Carolyn Tate is finishing a novel, "In the Land of One Death." A Professor Emerita of Pre-Columbian art history (Texas Tech University), she published two academic books: *Reconsidering Olmec Visual Culture: The Unborn, Women, and Creation* and *Yaxchilan: The Design of a Maya Ceremonial City.*

Pam Tucker has been published in *Trestlecreek Review*, *Literary Mama*, and *Encore*. She is the author of the children's book *Paper Monsters.* In 2018, her poetry won honorable mention in the Utah Division of Arts and Museums Original Writing Competition. She splits her time between Oregon and Utah.

Ted Virts retired to Bend on his daughter's recommendation. She mentioned, since he was old and still played outside, doctors were available for predictable injuries or ailments. Thus assured, Ted spends his time biking, writing, and playing ukulele. He enjoys his wife's friendship and her strange new interest in birding.

Ellen Waterston is the author of four poetry and three nonfiction titles. *Walking the High Desert*, UW Press, is her most recent nonfiction. She is founder of the Writing Ranch and the Waterston Desert Writing Prize. She serves on the faculty of the OSU-Cascades Low-Residency MFA in Creative Writing.

Joseph A. White Jr. has lived and traveled worldwide but chose the Pacific Northwest to raise his family and pursue his careers in telecommunications and industrial safety education. "The Between State," the first in a series of science fiction novels, is scheduled for release in late 2022. "The Beach" is his first short story.

Randy Workman is a Central Oregon writer whose essays, articles, and poetry have appeared in various publications including *Placed: An Encyclopedia of Central Oregon, Vol. 1, Los Angeles Daily News Sunday Magazine*, Toner Mishap, *The Seattle Times*, and *433* magazine.

Made in the USA
Coppell, TX
12 November 2022

86215554R00142